PROJECT LEARNING WITH 3D PRINTING

3D Printing at School and Makerspaces

KEON ARASTEH BOOZARJOMEHRI

Cavendish Square
New York

Published in 2018 by Cavendish Square Publishing, LLC
243 5th Avenue, Suite 136, New York, NY 10016

First Edition

Website: cavendishsq.com

Library of Congress Cataloging-in-Publication Data

Names: Boozarjomehri, Keon Arasteh, author.
Title: 3D printing at school and makerspaces / Keon Arasteh Boozarjomehri.
Description: New York : Cavendish Square Publishing, [2018] | Series: Project learning with 3D printing | Includes bibliographical references and index.
Identifiers: LCCN 2017022972 (print) | LCCN 2017024264 (ebook) | ISBN 9781502631497 (E-book) | ISBN 9781502631480 (library bound) | ISBN 9781502634269 (pbk.)
Subjects: LCSH: Three-dimensional printing--Juvenile literature. | Student activities--Juvenile literature.
Classification: LCC TS171.95 (ebook) | LCC TS171.95 .B66 2018 (print) | DDC 621.9/88--dc23
LC record available at https://lccn.loc.gov/2017022972

Editorial Director: David McNamara
Editor: Fletcher Doyle
Copy Editor: Nathan Heidelberger
Associate Art Director: Amy Greenan
Designer: Alan Sliwinski
Production Coordinator: Karol Szymczuk
Photo Research: J8 Media

The photographs in this book are used by permission and through the courtesy of: Cover, p. 48 Asiseeit/E+/Getty Images; Back cover Jonathan Juursema/Wikimedia Commons/File:Felix 3D Printer - Printing Head.JPG/CC BY SA 3.0; p. 4 Laboratory/Alamy Stock Photo; p. 8 Anna Webber/Getty Images for Academy of Motion Picture Arts and Sciences; p. 11 Wsfs/Shutterstock.com; p. 14 Cristina M. Fletes/St. Louis Post-Dispatch/TNS/Getty Images; p. 21, 23, 26 , 28, 29, 34, 38, 42, 45, 59, 61, 68 74 , 76 , 78, 80, 88, 94, 96, 98, 101, 103, 109 Keon Boozarjomehri; p. 55 Artyom Geodakyan/TASS/Getty Images; p. 66 Science Photo/Shutterstock.com; p. 90 Carlo Amoruso/Taxi/Getty Images; p. 92 Monkey Business Images/Shutterstock.com.

Printed in the United States of America

CONTENTS

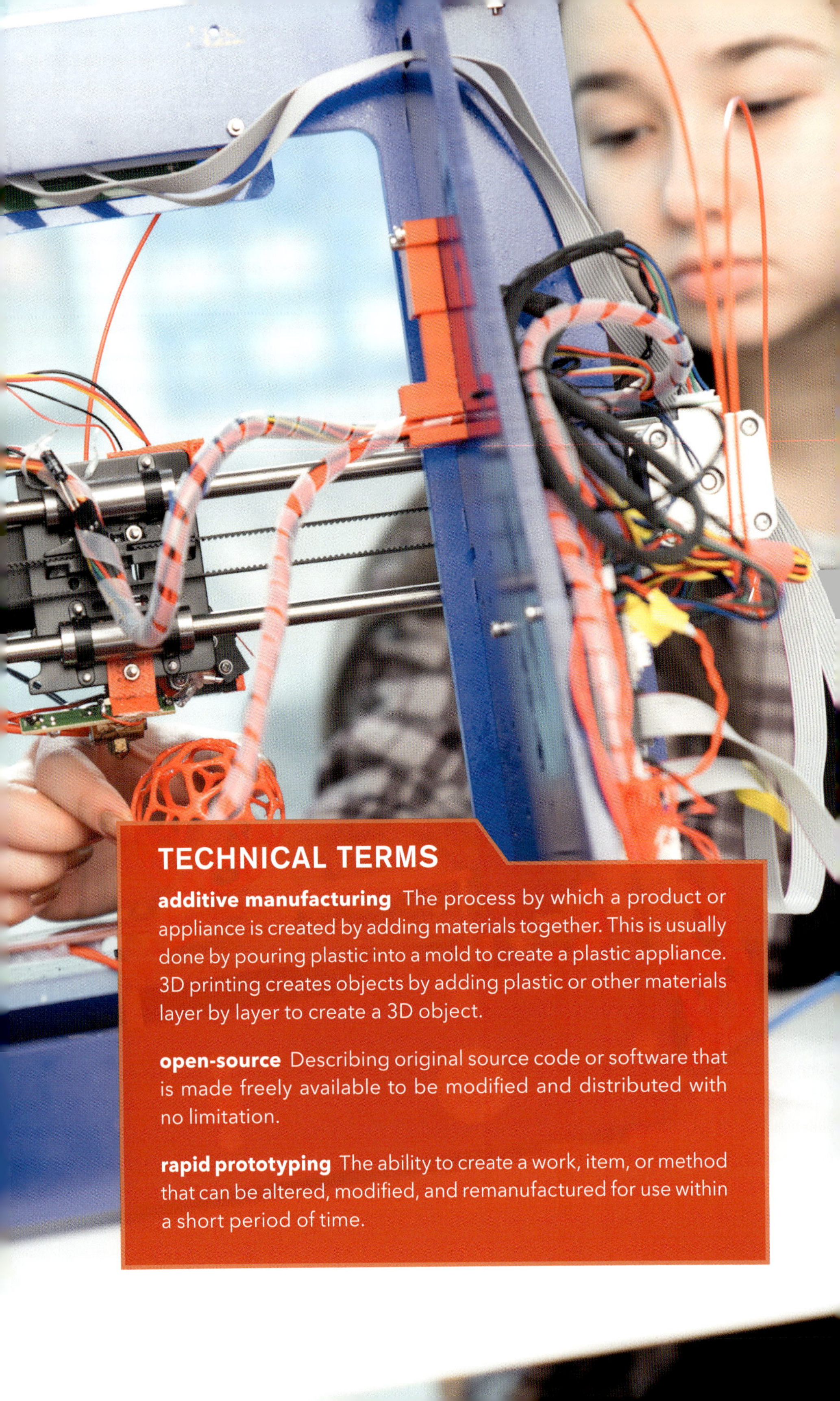

TECHNICAL TERMS

additive manufacturing The process by which a product or appliance is created by adding materials together. This is usually done by pouring plastic into a mold to create a plastic appliance. 3D printing creates objects by adding plastic or other materials layer by layer to create a 3D object.

open-source Describing original source code or software that is made freely available to be modified and distributed with no limitation.

rapid prototyping The ability to create a work, item, or method that can be altered, modified, and remanufactured for use within a short period of time.

CHAPTER ONE

Background and Tools

SCHOOLS AND COMMUNITIES ARE SETTING UP MAKERSPACES to give students access to technology that will allow them to create. There is an emphasis on play, so that students can have fun while learning skills they will need for college and in the working world.

These facilities make this technology more accessible and cost effective so families and makers can get started creating. Among the most useful pieces in a makerspace is a 3D printer. While the purpose of a makerspace is to allow students to learn while doing it themselves, often students are required to attend an introductory workshop before using the equipment on their own. This

Opposite: Makerspaces give young people a chance to get hands-on experience with a 3D printer.

book is intended to be that workshop. It will get you started on your DIY journey.

A 3D printer works in a simple fashion. There are three main methods that 3D printers use to print. These are the most popular and viable methods to print, but they vary a lot. They involve using either resin, lasers, or heating elements. These all achieve creating a 3D model by stacking layers to create an object. This is called **additive manufacturing**, in which you create something by adding materials to it until there is a final product. Although 3D printing is incredibly popular and seems like cutting-edge technology, it has been around for longer than you might think. The technology has been growing since the 1980s.

In 1980, Dr. Hideo Kodama made the first attempt at 3D printing. He used a technique called SLA printing, which stands for "stereolithography apparatus" printing. "Stereo" means "from several sources," and "lithography" means "light emission," so "stereolithography" means "emitting light from several sources." This technique uses ultraviolet (UV) light to solidify photosensitive resin in a resin bath. This requires setting a **build plate** in a bath of resin and projecting light through the resin from above or below onto the plate in a precise manner. By projecting the light at certain angles, the resin solidifies on the plate, creating the first layer. Then the plate is lifted or lowered layer by layer in the bath. As it moves, the UV light projects and solidifies more layers onto the already solidified resin. Thus, a 3D model is printed once all the layers are complete and the 3D model is lifted out of the resin bath. This technology was far ahead of its time and is just now becoming commercially accessible. The most popular consumer-grade SLA printer is called the Form 2, and this printer can create 3D prints in a fraction of the time it takes a regular 3D printer. However, it is far more complicated and requires professional maintenance. Therefore, it is rarely available for use by students.

Tool for Animation

Though Dr. Kodama was the first to attempt SLA printing, he was not the first to succeed and patent the technology. Charles Hull beat him to it in 1986. Hull would go on to found the 3D Systems Corporation. It would release the first SLA printer, called SLA-1, in 1987.

After Hull capitalized on SLA printing, Carl Deckard patented the first selective laser sintering (SLS) technology at the University of Texas in 1988. This technique requires two things: a high-powered laser, and a large solid source of powder grains. This form of printing requires shooting a laser at the powder source. The laser will fuse this powder wherever it is shot. Just as with the SLA printer, the SLS printer goes layer by layer to create its model. This form of printing is incredibly precise and can create beautiful models. The animation studio Laika uses this form of 3D printing to create its stop-motion characters. The animators create and pose them, then color print them with an SLS printer. This allows them to make a 3D character in software that can be posed and printed repeatedly to achieve stop-motion movement. Among the movies they have made are *Coraline*, *The Boxtrolls*, and *Kubo and the Two Strings*. Since the laser, powder, and quality of these printers need to be quite fine, they are usually very expensive, starting at several thousand dollars for the printer alone.

The most popular and cost-effective 3D printing technique is called fused deposition modeling (FDM). This is probably the type of printer that will be available at your school or in the makerspace. Scott Crump (cofounder of Stratasys, Ltd.) patented this printing method in 1992. Since modern consumer 3D printers use FDM-style printing, they are far more easy to use. The printers that we will be working with throughout

Laika printed this stop-motion character for its film *The Boxtrolls*. The character can be printed in many poses to create movement.

this book are FDM printers. They use motors to move a nozzle that dispenses plastic on a plate. This plastic sticks to the plate and creates what is called a layer. The printer continues to dispense plastic until the first layer is complete.

Once the first layer is finished, the motors move the nozzle slightly higher to start work on the second layer. The printer dispenses more plastic onto the first layer to make the second layer. Once the second layer is finished, the printer moves on to the third layer, and so on. The 3D printer lays plastic one layer at a time so that the plastic is set in a stable way. Once the plastic is cooled, the printer can move on to the following layers and create the 3D-printed piece. Some 3D models have hundreds of layers, and these are dependent on settings that you assign to the 3D model.

Testing Designs

Through the 1990s, there was an increase in the use of 3D printing for corporate creations, and 3D printing became more and more efficient. The most useful quality of 3D printing became gradual, low-cost modification. This is the ability to change a product during its production cycle. When something is created, like a cup, toy, or part, it undergoes a production life cycle. This begins with identifying the purpose of the item, then planning the item, executing that plan by creating the item, and then assessing some issues to address for the next cycle. The creation of the item from the plan is usually a strict process.

Let's work through an example. If you want to make a cup holder for a car for production, you first measure the cup you want it to hold, and then you create an adapter for the car. This is done with software to create a model that will eventually become the product. However, the shape can sometimes be an approximation. Therefore, if you're making a cup holder, it is a good idea to take the most common-sized cup and measure it. Then, using those measurements, you can develop a piece that fits the bottom of that cup so it works for most cups. This can be problematic depending on the measurements taken, the tolerances of the manufacturing materials, and the model's complexity, These all can affect the final product. After making the model, it is sent to a factory to be made into a mold. This mold is ready for final production, so the company can create hundreds of those cup holders in a short amount of time.

Because of the specificity that measurements and designs need to incorporate, there is a chance for error in any one of those measurements. One error can ruin the entire model. Creating a mold for production is incredibly expensive. Some molds can cost up to $10,000. This is mostly because those molds are durable and made for mass production. But, if that mold is faulty in any way, that is a huge cost to an otherwise smooth production. So, if you get the diameter of the cup holder wrong, that is a $10,000 cost and another trip to the design studio to fix the mistake.

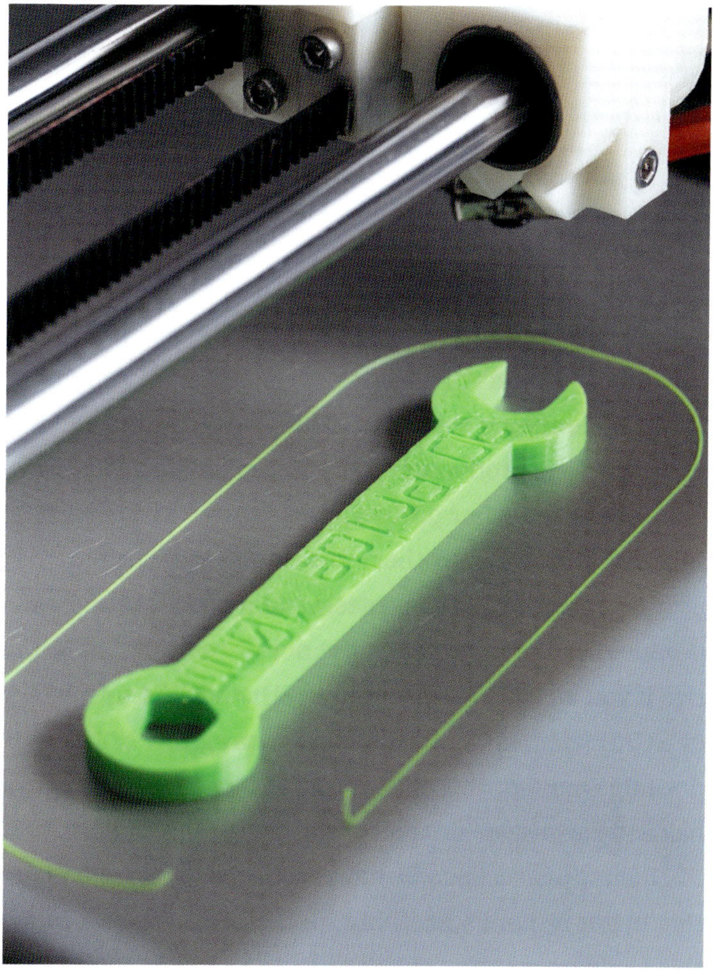

You can 3D print a prototype for a wrench that can tighten and loosen hexagonal screws and nuts on your 3D printer.

This is where 3D printing comes in handy. After the design process, you can ensure that your cup holder fits your cup by 3D printing the prototype. When you have the 3D model, you can send it to the 3D printer to create the first prototype within a few hours. Use this prototype most economic factors of 3D printing is the materials; 1 kilogram (2.2 pounds) of plastic usually costs between $15 and $40. With that much material, one can create at least two prosthetic limbs, depending on the size and density. Moreover, 3D printing is incredibly useful for quickly creating and supporting new, exciting items even before they are released for measurement. Some makerspaces charge for the **filament** you use while

A young girl who has just received a 3D-printed prosthetic forearm shakes hands with an excited friend.

printing your project. With the low cost of materials, students can experiment without spending a lot of money.

An example of how successful this prototyping method has become is Boeing using advanced 3D printers to create parts for its planes. Since the manufacturing of planes is such a long and specialized process, it is the perfect scenario to incorporate 3D printing. Boeing uses an industrial-grade metal 3D printer to create strong custom metal parts. Since there is a limited number of each airplane model, and these pieces are made specifically for those planes, 3D printing can reduce production costs by millions of dollars. Instead of creating a large production line for these parts, Boeing can create a specific amount that are perfectly fitted for its planes. A 3D printer is becoming one of the most valuable assets for creating custom devices for a limited minting. So let's start preparing to print!

Preparing for Printing

Most 3D printers will need to be calibrated after they are taken out of their shipping box. This is done to ensure they will print your project accurately. Calibration will usually be done by a supervisor at school or in a community makerspace. However, if you are lucky enough to be around when a new 3D printer arrives, ask to help with the calibration. This will give you a chance to learn a lot about how that printer works.

Before you can get started 3D printing, you should ensure you have all the right tools to make something amazing the first time. Though the 3D printer is an amazing tool in itself, it cannot do its job without the items to maintain it. At makerspaces, even ones at school, there usually is no maintenance person around to help you should something go wrong while you are working on a project. Therefore, it is good to learn some basic maintenance before you start to play.

There are several tools that are necessary and some that are optional. All the following tools should come in handy when working with a 3D printer. If these tools are not available at the makerspace, consider bringing in your own.

The first and most important tool is a putty knife. This a small spatula-type device with a flat metal end that fans out of a small handle. This small knife is your primary way to free your 3D prints from the printer. The 3D printer uses filament (or the melted plastic) to create a 3D print. However, when the filament is laid on the build plate (the plate where the 3D print is made), it must adhere (or stick) strongly. This will make sure that the model does not move and can be consistently built upon. Therefore, once the 3D print is finished, it will still be firmly stuck to the build plate.

This is where the putty knife comes in. You must wedge the putty knife like a spatula between the build plate and the 3D print. Once wedged, simply apply pressure upward to free the 3D print from the build plate little by little. To begin to wedge the putty knife between the 3D print and the build plate, simply push the sharp corner of the knife under a corner of the 3D print and wiggle it under the print more and more. Another method to wedge the knife is to chisel away at the base of the 3D print. This will eventually dig under the 3D print and allow for you to free the print.

In either case, be careful! When chiseling the print or wedging the putty knife under the print, make sure your non-wedging hand is at a safe distance or away from the direction of your putty knife. It has become a joke among the 3D printing community that unintentionally stabbing your non-wedging hand is a "rite of passage" in 3D printing.

3D PRINTING TIP

Wear gloves to shield your hands when removing a print from the build plate. Also be aware of the pressure and force you are applying to the putty knife to lessen any danger in case of a slip.

Make sure to be incredibly careful when doing any work on your 3D printer. Removing a 3D print, handling the **extruder**, and fixing motors or the nozzle can all be dangerous, so please be cautious and focused.

The putty knife is essential for 3D printing, but maintenance is also incredibly important. The first important maintenance tool is a screwdriver. Most people have a Phillips screwdriver (cross head), but many 3D printers use different types of screws. For example, several of the popular Prusa i3 3D printers are held together with hex-bit screws. This is a screw bit that has a hexagon as the locking mechanism instead of the cross that a Phillips screw has. If your 3D printer uses one style of screw that is consistent throughout, there are usually different sizes of that screw used. Because of this, we recommend getting a multi-bit screwdriver. These are screwdrivers that have several interchangeable heads that allow you to screw or unscrew several different types and sizes of screw with only one handle.

Extruder: The Hot Spot

Sometimes you might need to replace some parts on your 3D printer, so in addition to a multi-bit screwdriver, it's good to have a wrench or two. The main use of a wrench is to tighten or loosen something on the printer that might be causing an issue or need replacing. Problems are most often found in the extruder nozzle. This is the place where the plastic comes out to be added to the print. After thousands of hours of printing, that nozzle will receive some wear and tear.

If you need to replace the extruder nozzle, the makerspace may have spares on hand. Replacing the extruder nozzle on some 3D printers is not a hard process, and you can do it yourself in most cases. However, you will need two types of wrenches. The first one is a socket wrench with a head that perfectly fits your nozzle. The nozzles are hexagonal (six sided), so a socket wrench with the measure of your nozzle should tighten or loosen the nozzle. You will also need an adjustable wrench. These are wrenches that allow you to adjust the width of the grip. You use the adjustable wrench to hold the other parts of the extruder. Using these two wrenches, you can hold the extruder assembly with the adjustable wrench and loosen or tighten the nozzle for replacement with the socket wrench. It is always a good idea to be prepared in case of a problem like this, so in addition to having these wrenches, it is advised to also have a spare extruder nozzle just in case. Make sure to order one that is the same width and size as the one your printer comes with, so it will be a quick and easy replacement.

Since we're talking about the nozzle where the plastic comes out, it is a good idea to have a steel wool brush next to your 3D printer. These brushes look just like a toothbrush but are made of steel wool. This makes them incredibly useful for cleaning your 3D printer's nozzle. The nozzle gets extremely hot and dispenses the plastic for your print. However, if the plastic does not lie properly, it can twist upward onto the nozzle and extruder assembly. This will cause plastic to gunk up the extruder. By using a steel wool brush, you can clean that plastic away quickly and effectively without endangering yourself or your other tools by touching the extremely hot nozzle.

Dislodging Jams

Finally, you should be prepared for times when the extruder jams. Jamming happens when the plastic that comes out does not melt and get dispensed properly. Therefore it gets stuck in the extruder. This is a common issue. The most severe is a jam in the extruder hot end. This means that the plastic is jammed between the heating section and the nozzle. It is hard to see the plastic when it is jammed this way, but it is definitely there and is causing a severe issue. The way to fix this type of jam is by using a thin, long, and strong piece of metal to push the plastic through the nozzle. We will push it through by pressing this long, thin piece of metal into the hole where we insert the filament. This will force the jammed plastic out of the nozzle and unjam the extruder. But be careful: this is a dangerous process because you need the nozzle and extruder to be hot enough to melt the plastic. An unfolded paperclip can work in a pinch, but we advise that you use a smaller pin-type tool that you can order.

Needle-nose pliers are a useful tool to keep you from getting hurt when clearing these jams. Needle-nose pliers are small pliers that have long and thin gripping sections. These are useful for holding on to your unjamming pin. You simply use the pliers to hold the pin and then insert and remove the pin several times until you see the jammed plastic come out of the nozzle. This helps to make sure that your hand is farther away from the heat source so you don't get burned.

Use pliers and a safety pin to unjam a 3D printer by pushing the jammed plastic through the extruder.

These pliers are useful for freeing another jam. If the plastic is jammed but is still poking out of the top of the extruder, you can use the needle-nose pliers to grasp the jammed plastic. Then you can apply constant and firm pressure outward to the plastic jamming the extruder, and after about thirty seconds, your plastic should be freed. The heat allows for the plastic to melt and stretch out, making it easier to pull out. Once freed, you can then insert more plastic and try printing again. You will know the printer is back to normal if it is dispensing plastic as usual. Needle-nose pliers are also good for inserting the plastic. When inserting filament into the extruder, you will need to make sure that it goes in consistently. Holding the plastic with the pliers and slowly inserting it will help you not jam the extruder and nozzle. If you press too hard or imprecisely, you can create a jam.

These pliers are also useful for working on your 3D-printed model as well. They will allow you to fix 3D prints as well as parts of the 3D printer. Though it is not recommended, you can use a pair of pliers to leverage a 3D print and pry it from the build plate. By doing so, you might break or damage your 3D print. We recommend using the putty knife for all 3D print removal needs. However, pliers show their utility when working on the 3D printer. Pliers can be used to tweak the 3D printer's motors and keep them working well. We will explore the use of pliers in the chapter about maintaining the 3D printer. A pair of pliers is also useful to have for post-printing needs.

When preparing your 3D model in software you can ensure that the print will work well by using what are called **supports**. Supports make sure that the 3D model will come out exactly as it has been planned in the software. These supports are small towers that are built from the build plate up to a part of the 3D model that needs the support during printing. Not all 3D prints will need supports. These supports, though thin, become their own structure that you need to remove from your print when it is completed. With the use of the pliers you can effectively remove the supports. It is advised to use needle-nose pliers. Their long prongs can get into the small areas to grip and pull away any supports.

In addition to pliers, it is a good idea to have a file kit or sandpaper. This especially helps for the supports we just mentioned. When supports are removed from a 3D print, they will almost always leave a small protrusion on the outside of the print where the supports were

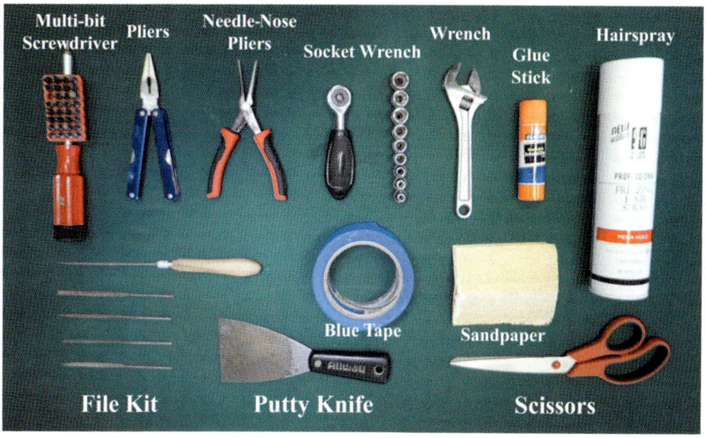

These are some of the useful tools you should keep around when using a 3D printer.

attached. This can be an issue if you want to make sure that your print does not have these protrusions and looks how it was designed. By using sandpaper and a file kit, you can slowly sand away the imperfections that supports leave. Simply rub the sandpaper against the area that was supported.

Sandpaper Selection

You should have sandpaper of several grits. The grit indicates the size of the grains of sand on the paper. A lower grit means the grains are larger. These grains can take more extra material or inconsistency away in a shorter time. The higher-numbered sandpaper has more sand grains per inch, and therefore the grains are smaller. So when using a higher-grit sandpaper, it takes a lot of pressure and time to remove material. However, higher-grit sandpaper is good for creating an incredibly smooth finish. It is also better when just a little bit of material needs to be removed or when you are working on fine details. The workflow that we use when treating a 3D print is starting with between 80- and 100-grit sandpaper to remove imperfections. Then use 200-grit sandpaper to keep consistency of the surface. Then finally, use 300-grit sandpaper to make the final product smooth.

Just like sandpaper, a file kit can help remove unwanted imperfections and get your prints to the quality you want. A file kit is a group of files (like a nail file) shaped like chop sticks. These metal files can get in very tight places to file down some imperfections or supports. Though you might only need one file, we recommend getting a file kit so you have files for almost every situation. File kits have files that are better suited for certain contours or shapes of your prints. And just like the sandpaper, the files that come in these kits are usually of different grits and can therefore be better suited for the quality of smoothness you are looking for.

Now that we have some tools to maintain your printer and finish a 3D print, let's make sure the 3D print will print perfectly the first time. As we will cover in the section on filaments, the plastic needs to stick to the build plate incredibly well. If it does not, then your 3D print will come out with print errors or not print at all. Leaving a printer to run a failed print can cause damage to your printer. To make sure this does not occur, it is crucial that you gather several items to make sure your 3D print will stick to the build plate. Blue painter's tape, glue, and hairspray will help your 3D print stick to the build plate. If these seem like random items, we will explain in more detail in the section on filament.

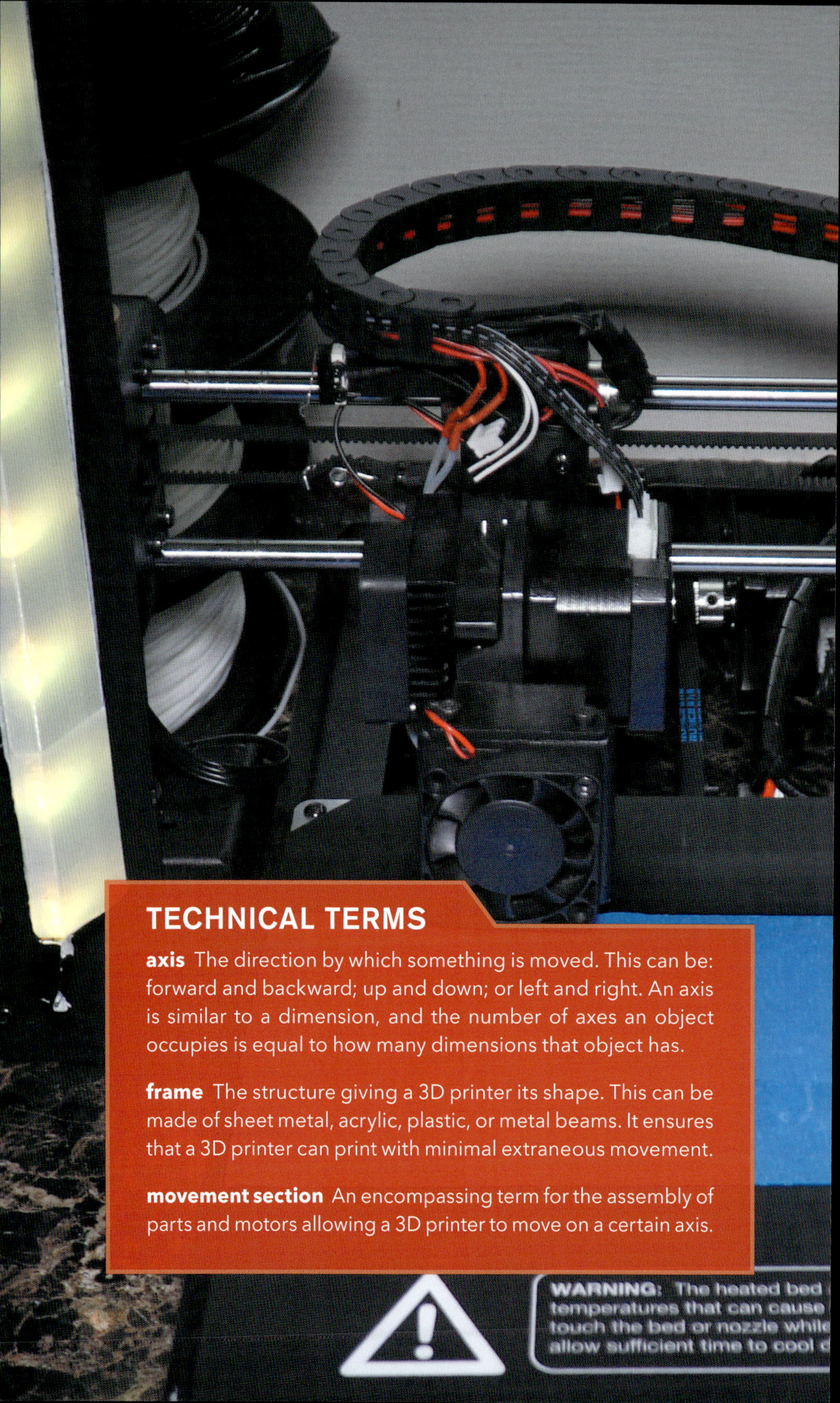

TECHNICAL TERMS

axis The direction by which something is moved. This can be: forward and backward; up and down; or left and right. An axis is similar to a dimension, and the number of axes an object occupies is equal to how many dimensions that object has.

frame The structure giving a 3D printer its shape. This can be made of sheet metal, acrylic, plastic, or metal beams. It ensures that a 3D printer can print with minimal extraneous movement.

movement section An encompassing term for the assembly of parts and motors allowing a 3D printer to move on a certain axis.

CHAPTER TWO

Getting Started

BEFORE YOU GET BEHIND THE WHEEL, LET'S LEARN HOW THE 3D printer works. Once you know how the printer works, troubleshooting any problems becomes second nature, and diagnosing issues feels fun! Also, your time on the printer may be limited in a makerspace, so knowing how it works will leave you more time to play. As with anything you learn, you have to learn the parts to know the whole. In math, for example, you learned numbers before you learned how to add, subtract, and multiply them. So let's start with the big parts.

Take a look at your elbow. Move your arm around and see how it works. As you can probably tell, there are a lot

Opposite: The Prusa i3 is a common 3D printer used in schools and makerspaces.

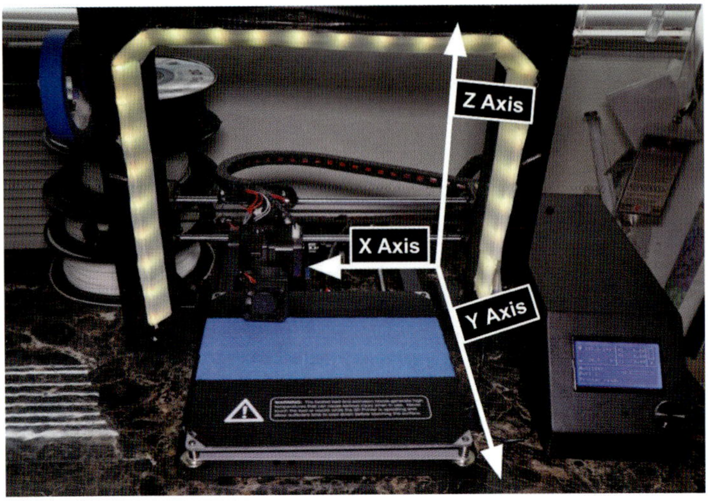

The three axes of movement allow the printer to work in all three dimensions.

of interworking parts. The muscles help you move your arm. The bones help it stay rigid. And the tendons keep the whole thing together. 3D printers are very similar. They use interworking parts that move together to make an object. As the brain drives the arm to move and pick things up, the 3D printer uses a small computer board to move motors and create an object. Just like the bones, muscles, and tendons of an arm, a 3D printer uses a **frame**, motors, and **pulleys** to move.

Just like building a hobby model or a toy set, it is important to know the parts that make a device. By knowing these, you can maintain your 3D printer and feel confident working on it. The first thing to note about a 3D printer is its frame. Many types of 3D printers use different materials to make a frame, and different housings to ensure that the frame is not tampered with during printing.

A common frame used by many manufacturers and hobbyists is called the Prusa i3. The Prusa i3 frame is easy to replicate, takes up little space, and is simple. This makes it very appealing to the 3D printing community. The Prusa i3 frame consists of three sections: the base, the vertical assembly, and the electronics. These sections utilize the extruder, build plate, and motors to create a 3D model.

Movement Sections

The base is the large rectangular section at the bottom of the 3D printer. It consists of a build plate, a motor,

These are the three movement sections (*x*, *y*, and *z* movement sections) of an FDM 3D printer.

and a pulley. The build plate is the plate on which the 3D-printed object will be created. It is sometimes called a bed plate. When 3D printing, you must be aware of the maximum size for your object. The maximum area of the build plate and the maximum height of the *z* **axis** define how big your 3D print can be. The motor drives the build plate. It is below the plate and attached via the pulley system. By using the pulley belt to move the build plate, the 3D printer can print forward and backward on the build plate. Forward and backward is referred to as the *y* axis. This is the first of the three dimensions in which the 3D printer can print.

The vertical assembly is the tall rectangle that goes from the base of the 3D printer upward. This defines the maximum height that you can make your 3D-printed model. The vertical assembly contains two sections, the *z* **movement section** and the *x* movement section. The *z* movement section is fairly simple. It is made up of two motors and two **threaded rods** only. This is the vertical frame that rises from the *y* movement base we just covered. These threaded rods move another section up and down, thus covering the *z*-axis movement. "Threaded" means that the rod has a "thread" like a screw, which allows for it to spin and screw into and out of something. Each motor has a threaded rod inserted into it. As the motors rotate, they move another section of the printer: the *x* movement section. The threads on the rods allow the *x* movement section to rise and fall on the vertical assembly in a controlled way. This gives us the upward and downward movement on the build plate. This is known as the *z* axis, and it gives the *z* movement section its name and function.

The final axis of movement is achieved by the *x* movement section we just mentioned. This section consists of a motor, pulley, and extruder assembly. The motor is attached to the extruder assembly in a similar way to the build plate being attached to the motor on the base. Therefore, the motor drives the extruder assembly using the pulley. It moves left to right, which is the *x* axis. This is then moved up and down, using the *z* movement section. And since the base controls moving the build plate forward and back, the build plate can now be utilized in all three axes.

But what is the extruder assembly? This is where all the magic happens. The extruder assembly is a package consisting of a fan, motor, and heating element. The motor feeds plastic into the heating element, which melts the plastic. Once the plastic is melted, the 3D printer can move in all three axes and lay it down to make a 3D model. The fan in the extruder assembly blows cool air onto the plastic that is laid down. Cooling the plastic makes it stay in the position in which it is laid. This will allow the plastic to stick to the build plate and to itself. The first layer is laid on the build plate, and as the printer lays more and more plastic, it creates more layers. This eventually makes the final 3D model. A finished plastic 3D model that is 3 inches (7.6 centimeters) tall can take forty layers of plastic to create.

Project Coordinator

Finally, we have the brain of the 3D printer: the electronics. The electronics consist of a computer board, power supply, and a motor driver board. The computer board is the brain to move the printer's muscles, which are really motors. The major difference between your brain and the printer's is that its has limited programming. It is only used to take in a digital model design and drive the motors to turn that design into a 3D-printed model. Since the computer board is only used to interpret data and does not have enough energy **throughput** (the amount of items or materials passing through a system or process) to power the motors, it communicates with the motor driver board. The driver board supplies power to the motors and allows them to move when the computer board asks them to. Finally, the power supply connects to an outlet to draw and regulate power throughout the 3D printer. It gives power to the computer board and to the motor driver board so the printer can think and move.

That was a quick overview of the main components of the 3D printer, so let's do a quick review. The *y*-axis movement section is the frame at the base of the printer. It moves the bed forward and backward. Next, we have the *z* movement section, which consists of the vertical frame, motors, and (threaded) rods that allow for the extruder and *x* movement section to move up and down. Finally, we have the *x* movement section, which rides on

3D PRINTING TIP

The best way to picture the three movement sections is by thinking of diagramming on graph paper. Looking from above, the *x* and *y* axes are like drawing a 90-degree angle on the build plate. *Y* moves forward and backward on the build plate, like the vertical line on the graph. *X* moves left and right along the base of the graph. And *z* moves outwardly from the build plate. This gives those two dimensions full shape into the third dimension.

the *z* axis threaded rods. This section consists of more motors and pulleys that move the extruder assembly left and right. The extruder is the block that melts and lays the plastic on the build plate, thus allowing a 3D print to be made. The extruder can move in two axes of the three-dimensional movement (*x* and *z* axes), while the build plate moves on the third axis (the *y* axis) below it. This allows for the plastic to be placed on the entire surface of the print bed and above it. Now that you know how a 3D printer moves its components to 3D print a model, you will be able to understand which parts are the most important of those components and how to ensure that the 3D printer is running smoothly.

We have shown that the 3D printer has to move along three axes to make a 3D model. It uses the three movement axes to achieve this three-dimensional movement. However, these different movement groups need their own maintenance to make sure your printer is running smoothly. Your ability to do any maintenance will be affected by how much access you have to your printer's pieces. If you are working on a prebuilt printer,

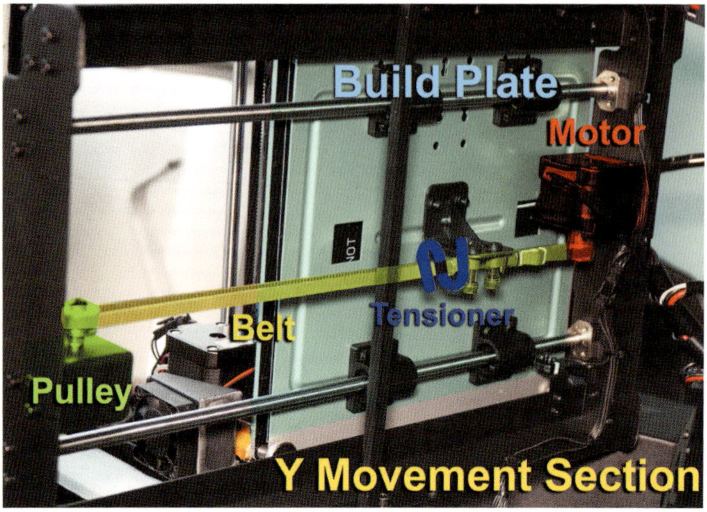

The different parts that make up the *y* movement section are hard to access beneath the build plate.

then you have a little less ability to improve or change your printer. If you have a printer that comes in a kit, you will have a few more maintenance options.

In both prebuilt and kit 3D printers, the *y* movement section is hard to adjust. This is because it is the most regulated section of the 3D printer. It is under the printer, so there are not many ways to access it. Depending on your printer, it might be easy to see or completely covered by a housing and therefore very hard to see. The main things to be aware of are the pulleys. If you look at the front and back of the base, you can probably see a motor in the back and a pulley in the front, or vice versa. This is how the *y* movement section achieves the forward-backward movement. The motor is connected to the front pulley by a rubber belt. When the motor turns, the rubber belt moves like a conveyor belt at a supermarket. Just as with a supermarket conveyor belt, a motor turns and allows whatever is resting on the belt to move either forward or backward. But instead of moving your groceries backward or forward, this conveyor belt moves your build plate forward and backward. If you look under the build plate on page 34, you will see a small bracket with which the build plate is attached to the rubber belt. This makes it so the build plate moves whenever the rubber belt is moved. The rubber belt is very tight on the pulley and the motor, and therefore the motor does not need to move much for the plate to travel far. However, this puts some strain on the motor and can cause friction that results in damage.

Tighten Your Belt

To make sure your build plate is moving well, you must make sure the rubber belt is tight. Considering that there is not much access to the base of the 3D printer, this may become a more advanced step. Overall, making a change to the base pulley system might require someone with advanced knowledge of your 3D printer. Some 3D printers come with a belt that is cut to the tightness the manufacturers wanted. The way to test this tightness is feeling the belt. If the belt is tight enough that you need to push hard to move the belt more than a quarter of an inch (6 millimeters), the belt is good to go. However, if it is not, then you need to tighten it. The easiest method

3D PRINTING TIP

If your belt is in one piece, then we do not recommend tampering with it or cutting it to tighten it. If there is a small bracket that is holding the belt together, you can change the belt tension. These brackets are usually held together with a screw. If you loosen the screw, the belt will come loose. Then you can pull it together tighter to make sure the build plate is moving well. However, do not pull it too tight or you could damage the motor, as stated earlier.

for tightening the belt, one that anyone can do, is to get an S-shaped piece of plastic. This 3D S shape is useful because you can loop the rubber belt through it easily. By causing the belt to stretch over the S shape, the belt will be tighter without unscrewing or tampering with the sections of the printer base. This is a good model to 3D print for a quick and easy fix.

Now that we understand what pulls the build plate, let's talk about the build plate itself. If you look underneath the build plate, in addition to the bracket that attaches to the belt, you will see two cylinders. These cylinders have rods going through them that attach to the base of the 3D printer. These cylinders are called linear **bearings**. The word "linear" is used because they allow for movement in one axis (forward and backward). The word "bearing" means "movement." So together, "linear bearing" refers to one axis of movement. These bearings sit under the build plate and allow for very smooth movement forward and backward. However, the bearings can cause problems if not properly lubricated. If the bearings do not fit the rods they sit on, or if the rods they sit on are not smooth, then there will be a lot of friction between the rods and the bearings. This will cause the build plate to not move smoothly, and therefore the motor will have to work harder to move the build plate. This can wear out your motor quickly. You can notice this if you hear a scratching sound when you try to move the build plate.

If the rods that the bearings are riding on are not smooth, then that will require you to replace them. This entails taking the 3D printer base apart and reassembling it with smooth rods. This will require you to examine the manual that the 3D printer came with and follow those instructions. If the rods are smooth but the bearings are having a hard time moving on the rods, then you will want to use a lubricant to allow the bearings to ride smoothly. In the cylindrical middle of the bearings that meet the rods, there is a small sponge-like rock. This is where you should apply the lubricant. This area will absorb and use the lubricant for quite a while. You can also apply the lubricant to the sections of the rod where the bearing rides. Do not use WD-40 for lubrication. WD-40 is not a lubricant, and its effect will fade within minutes and dry what you sprayed it with.

With that, the major components of the *y* movement section are good to go. If you take a look, you can see a few knobs under the build plate that we have not covered. These are the **leveling** knobs; they control the level of the build plate. We will cover them more in chapter 5, when we're ready to print.

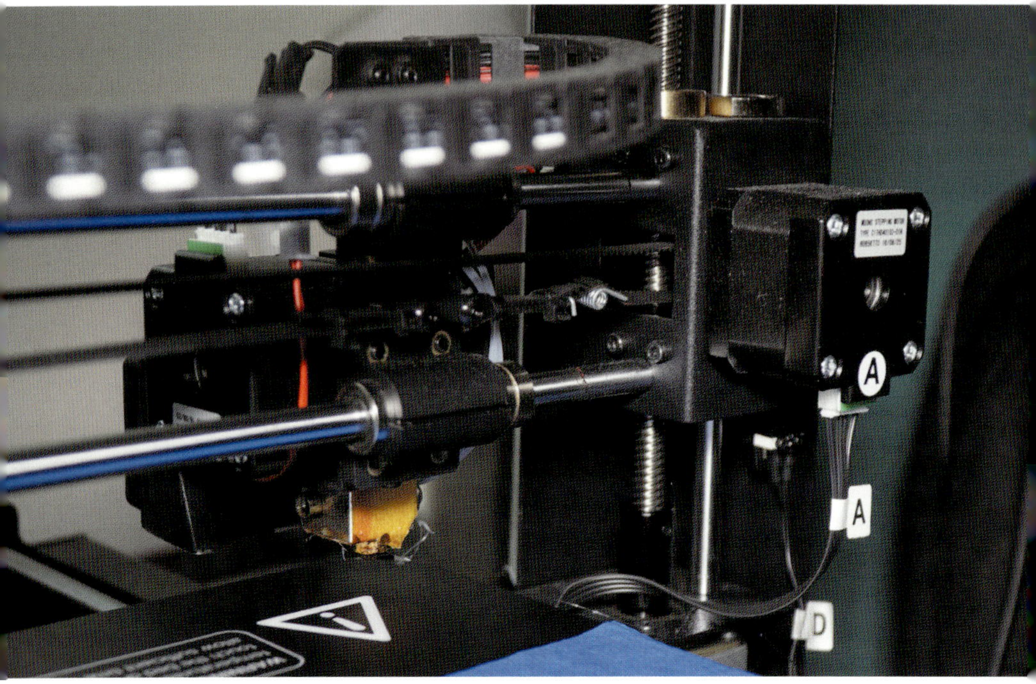

This small part of the *z* movement section is where the *x* movement section attaches to it. Note the threaded rod that spins to make the *x* movement section go up or down.

Connected Movements

The *z* movement section is the simplest section of the 3D printer. However, it might be one of the most important to keep calibrated. Since the *x* movement section rides on the *z* frame threaded rods, the *x* movement section relies on those threaded rods to work properly. You might ask, "Why does the *z* movement section have threaded rods, and not just smooth rods?" This is because the *x* movement section needs to move up and down the *z* frame. So the *x* movement section is attached to the *z* movement rods by threaded nuts. These nuts are screwed on the rods and help the *x* movement section rise and fall. This *z*-axis rising and falling happens when the motors (on the *z*-axis frame) rotate. Just like a screwdriver rotating a screw, the motors rotate the threaded rods and cause the nuts on the *x* movement section to go up or down the threaded rods. Therefore, the *x* movement section can perform a controlled rising and falling action.

The biggest issue that arises with the *z* movement frame is the balance of the *x* movement section. Since the *x* movement section sits across the threaded rods, its has to sit parallel to the build plate. This means that every part of the *x* movement section needs to be the exact same distance from the build plate at all times. This is extremely important because the *x* movement section lays the plastic. Therefore, if any part of the *x* movement section is offset from the build plate by any degree, then that offset portion of the *x* movement section will lay the plastic poorly. This issue is the most important part of 3D printing. If the first layer of your 3D-printed model is laid poorly, then the entire model may be compromised. To think of this in a statistical sense, the first 4 percent of most 3D printing processes can cause 80 percent of the issues. That 4 percent is the printer putting down the first layer, and it can compromise and ultimately ruin 100 percent of your 3D-printed model.

We can ensure that this error does not happen with a very simple process. Since the *x* movement section rides on the threaded rods, all we need to do is make sure that the *x* movement nuts on both threaded rods are at the same height. The easiest way to do this is to take a ruler and measure the distance from each side of the *x* movement section to the build plate or the surface on which the 3D printer is sitting. If both of the farthest sides (the areas where the bearings sit on the threaded rods) of the *x* movement section are the same distance from the build plate or surface, then congratulations, your *x* movement section is level and should lay the plastic consistently on the build plate!

However, if the two sides are not level, then we have some work to do. Which side of the *x* movement section is lower than the other? All you need to do is find whichever section is lower and twist the threaded rod on that side. If you twist the threaded rod clockwise, then that side of the *x* movement section will fall. If you twist the threaded rod counterclockwise, then that side of the *x* movement section will rise. You can remember this simply by taking your right fist and sticking your thumb up. If you twist your right hand in the direction of your fingers, then the *x* movement section will go in the direction of your thumb. For example, if you open your right hand then close your fingers, they should move counterclockwise and your thumb will be up. Therefore, the *x* movement section will rise if you twist the threaded rod that direction. In addition, if you point your thumb down and then close your fist, you will notice that your fingers will close clockwise. Therefore, the *x* movement section will go in the direction of your thumb, which is down. So twist the threaded rod of the lower section counterclockwise. This will allow it to rise. All you need to do now is twist the threaded rod until that side of the *x* movement section is as far from the build plate as the other side. Once both sides are the same height, then you've leveled the *x* movement section on your own! Now we're getting somewhere!

3D PRINTING TIP

The right hand rule can be applied to physics as well. If your thumb on your right hand is facing up, then when you twist a screw or apply torque to an object in the direction of your right hand's fingers, the object will travel upward. The same is true when you point your right thumb down.

Finally, we have the *x* movement section. This is, by far, the most important part of the 3D printer and will need the most maintenance while printing. This section consists of three major parts: the bearings that ride on the *z* frame, the rods that hold the horizontal assembly, and the extruder assembly that rides those horizontal rods.

The bearings that ride on the *z* frame need very little maintenance. Just like the bed assembly, they have bearings that sit on smooth rods. These bearings allow for linear movement up and down. As we just discussed, the *z* frame also has the threaded rods that drive the

x movement section up and down. To maintain this, we just need to lubricate the bearings and smooth rods on the z frame that support the x movement section. As with the build plate assembly, just lubricate the linear bearings by spraying lubricant into the bearings' spongy rock insides. These will absorb the lubricant so it can be used for an extended period of time. It is also a good idea to lubricate the smooth rods so there is little friction there, too. An additional step that will help your printer move smoothly is polishing the threaded rods. By doing this, the x movement section can ride up and down more easily, with less stress on the nuts that drive this movement. On this linear assembly, you might notice something familiar: there is a pulley on one side. This pulley is used by the extruder assembly to control the x movement. The rubber belt must be fairly tight to allow for efficient movement, just like the build plate rubber belt.

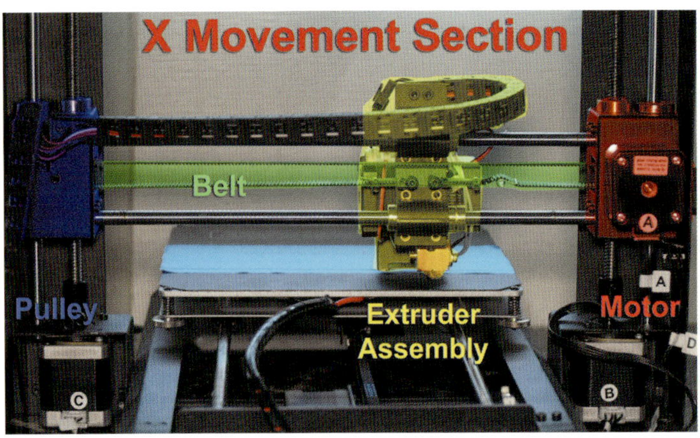

The parts that make up the x movement section control the movement of the extruder assembly.

Horizontal Assembly

Now we move on to the horizontal assembly. This is everything that sits on the *z* frame. It consists of the plastic sections that hold the linear bearings (riding on the *z* frame), the extruder assembly, and the two rods that the extruder assembly rides on. The two rods that support the extruder assembly are smooth rods, so they do not need much maintenance. Just like with the build plate and printer base, you need to ensure that the smooth rods do not have imperfections or bumps. This will cause friction and affect the movement of the extruder assembly. If there are bumps, these rods will need to be replaced. If there are no bumps, then good lubrication is the only thing that will help this section of the printer function. Simply lubricate the bearings that ride on the rods, as well as the rods themselves.

Finally, before we tackle the extruder assembly, we must assess the tightness of the pulleys that move the extruder assembly. Just as with the build plate pulleys, simply push or pull the belt to assess how tight it is. If it has little give, then there is no issue. If there is too much give, then you will need to apply the S-shaped plastic pieces, just as we did with the build plate belt. This is the safest way to increase the tension. There is a more advanced technique that requires taking the belt apart at its buckle, tightening it, then putting the belt and buckle back together. However, we do not recommend doing this yourself if you have only a beginner-level knowledge of

3D printers. Tell either a teacher or an administrator and let them make the adjustment.

The last thing to cover is by far the most important. The extruder assembly is crucial to the entire 3D printing process. The rest of the functions listed so far affect movement functionality. However, the extruder is the part the 3D printer is moving. It does the printing. The extruder assembly is where three main functions happen. The plastic is inserted, the plastic is heated to a melting temperature, and the plastic is extruded onto the build plate. Let's look at each of these functions.

First, we feed the plastic into the extruder. This plastic is called filament. The filament comes in many different materials. Each of them needs its own settings and heat levels to work well with a 3D printer. We will go over different kinds of filament more in chapter 3. Just like thread, 3D printing filament is wrapped around a thin cylinder called a **spool**. This spool is then suspended somewhere through its center hole. The 3D printer you work with should come prepackaged with a spool holder. When placed on the spool holder, the spool should be able to rotate freely. Just like a thread being fed into a sewing machine, the plastic is fed into the 3D printer so it can be laid by the extruder onto the build plate. It is fed into the extruder assembly. At the top of the extruder assembly is a small hole. This hole is where the filament is inserted. It feeds the filament into a motor. That motor then turns and pushes the filament into the hot end. The hot end melts the filament, which then comes out of the nozzle.

To feed the filament into the extruder assembly, there should be a small tab next to the hole. Pressing down on this tab unlocks the motor, which allows for the filament to be inserted. Once the filament is inserted and the tab is released, then the filament will be held in place, allowing the motor to feed it to the extruder.

To start feeding the filament, we recommend finding the "preheat" feature in your printer's menu. By preheating the printer for the plastic that you are using, you can then feed the filament into the extruder and see it coming out. This is a visual clue that your filament is not getting stuck in the motor. If your filament gets stuck, this is called a jam. It is easily remedied by unscrewing the extruder assembly. First, you must make sure that

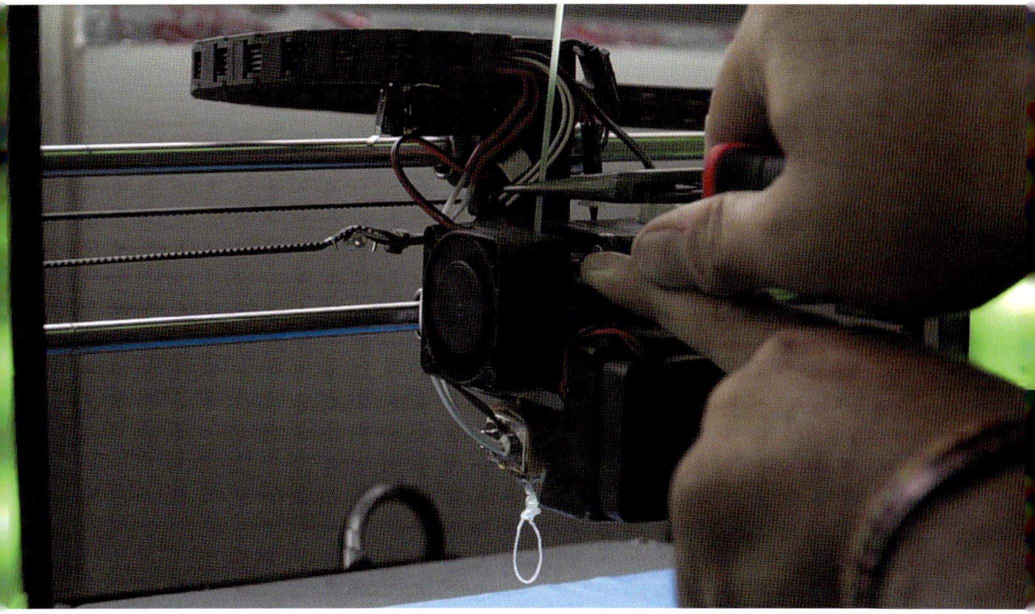

A tab is depressed while needle-nose pliers are used to feed filament into the extruder.

your printer is unplugged or turned off so that the hot end does not burn you. Then, unscrew the assembly. Be careful not to damage the fans; they are essential to cooling the plastic and must be replaced if damaged. Once the assembly is in pieces, you should be able to see the motor as a cross section. You can see how and where the motor feeds the filament into the hot end. Simply pull the filament out of the motor to unjam the printer.

A Bigger Mess

There is also a more extensive jamming that can occur with an extruder: a hot end jam. This occurs when the filament is fed into the hot end too quickly. This causes there to be too much filament in the hot end, and this will not allow any filament through the extruder. This can be remedied in one of three ways, each dependent on the way the filament is jammed. The first and easiest fix is pulling out the filament. This is only possible if the filament is sticking out of the extruder (where the motor feeds it in). You simply need to turn the printer on and preheat the hot end for that filament type. (Be very careful! It is extremely hot!) Then, using a set of pliers, apply consistent pressure outwards. After about ten seconds of the plastic heating up and your pliers pulling on the filament, the plastic will unjam and come free.

If the filament is jammed too far into the extruder, then you must free it by pushing the filament through the extruder. Do not try this by pushing more plastic

3D PRINTING TIP

Clean your extruder periodically so it will not jam often. Make sure your printer is off or cooled down if you do not need the hot end on.

through the extruder; this may cause a far more severe jam. Simply use a safety pin or long needle. By uncoiling the safety pin, you have created a long metal piece. This can be used to apply pressure to the back of the jammed filament. Preheat the extruder for the filament you are trying to unjam, and press the safety pin into the extruder hole. Please use pliers to push the safety pin in the extruder. It is extremely hot and can cause severe burns. After some pressure is applied, the filament should start to come through. If not, pull out the uncoiled safety pin and try again. Repeat until you see a good amount of your filament come through the extruder. Your extruder should now be fixed.

The last resort for fixing your extruder is purchasing a replacement extruder nozzle. Extruder nozzles are cheap and only require unscrewing the extruder nozzle and hose to remove. Then simply put the new nozzle and hose in place. Be sure that this new nozzle fits your printer and has the same hole size as your previous nozzle. This hole dictates to what fidelity you can print your 3D prints. After about one thousand hours of use, it may be a good idea to replace the nozzle because the extruder hole can become skewed from use and cause imperfect prints.

TECHNICAL TERMS

malleable Easily bent or shaped to fit a surface or position. Certain filaments can be more malleable when printing, which will ensure they stick to the build plate easier.

material mixing Adding materials such as metals to plastic filament. These metals will melt at a similar temperature to the plastic.

subtractive manufacturing A form of 3D printing in which material is cut away from, rather than added to, material on the build plate.

CHAPTER THREE

Printing Materials

JUST LIKE AN INK PRINTER USES INK TO PRINT ON PAPER, a school or makerspace 3D printer uses plastic (also known as filament) to print on its build plate. Instead of cartridges, 3D printers use spools of filament to feed the plastic into the printer. However, 3D printers can use several types of plastic to create a 3D model. The five major plastics that are used for 3D printing are ABS, PETG, PVA, PLA, and flexible filament. Not all 3D printers can print with all of these filaments, so check the user manual for which filament types your printer can handle. Each of these different types of filament has its own pluses and minuses. Though most 3D models can be

Opposite: Different types and shades of filament can add color to your 3D printing projects. The filament comes on spools that are mounted on the printer.

printed with any of these filament types, it is important to consider which filament (with which attributes) will help your print's function. After understanding each one of these filaments individually, you will know which one will help your 3D print the most.

ABS (which stands for acrylonitrile butadiene styrene) is the eldest brother to these filaments. It is the strongest of these five filaments and was the filament that hobbyist 3D printers used first. It can take the most stress in a 3D model. However, this also becomes an issue when printing. Though it might not be the hardest filament to work with, it can be hazardous. ABS can be printed at temperatures between 220 and 250 degrees Celsius (428 and 482 degrees Fahrenheit). The printing temperature is a big issue with ABS. Since the printing temperature is so high, the filament won't stick to a standard build plate. There must be a **heated bed** on the 3D printer to use ABS. The heated bed must be set to at least 100°C (212°F). This is to ensure that the filament is still **malleable** on the build plate. We will cover this in detail in the section about secondary printing aids. In addition to needing certain equipment, it is also harmful. It has been shown that ABS is semi-toxic. When heated and printed, it creates a faint gas that can cause health issues. For this reason, many schools and makerspaces do not buy it. However, if you are printing with ABS, make sure that there is a plexiglass shield or case over your 3D printer to keep the harmful gas away from your lungs.

Even with all these concerns, ABS is also one of the least reliable filaments to use. This is because of warping. Even after being printed well, the final model can be warped and might not fit the dimensions as created in your software. Since it is being put under the harshest conditions of all these filaments, that heat can make the layers that were already laid change from how they started. This is upsetting, based on how much effort ABS takes to print. However, the main benefit of ABS is that it is incredibly strong. ABS needing a higher printing temperature is a product of its strength. ABS, of all of these filaments, is the strongest while still being as lightweight as the other plastics. For printing things like quadcopters or other flying materials, ABS is a fair option. However, be wary of its flaws and issues.

Strong and Safe

PLA (polylactic acid) is the most popular plastic to print with. It is the type most commonly used at schools and makerspaces. Of these five popular plastics, PLA requires the lowest maintenance and is the easiest to use. The main reason it is so agreeable is that it has a low melting point. PLA can be melted and used for 3D printing at temperatures as high as 210°C (410°F). However, you can potentially melt PLA at 180°C (356°F) for 3D printing use. This is extremely low in comparison to the other printing plastics. PLA adheres well to the print plate and is less liable to warp and can be printed without a heated bed.

3D prints that are still strong. Flexible filament is a very interesting plastic, and it comes in many shapes and sizes. Many vendors have different cocktails for flexible filament. However, all are fairly hard to use and take a lot of tweaking. We consider flexible filament to be fairly advanced, and the settings to use for it depend on the vendor you purchase it from. Several flexible filaments can be printed using PLA print heat, while some others must be printed using PETG print settings. However, flexible filament becomes hard to use because of its flexible nature. This can cause it to get stuck in the extruder assembly. The motor that feeds the filament into the extruder is used to rigid filament. When flexible filament is introduced, it can get caught in the gears of the motor and jam the assembly. The only solution to this is taking apart the extruder assembly and manually removing the flexible filament from the gears. This can happen fairly often with flexible filament. The major way to overcome this is to make sure the flexible filament you purchase is fairly firm so it won't jam the extruder motor. But in addition to that issue, flexible filament is notorious for not adhering to the build plate. There are several very useful solutions to overcome the lack of bed plate cohesion that can help all filaments you can print with, especially PLA.

Keeping Its Cool

A standard secondary aid for 3D printing is a bed fan. This is a second fan below the main fan on the extruder assembly. The main fan cools the extruder as it lays plastic. This is necessary to control the heat of the extruder and help the plastic keep its structure coming out of the extruder. Though not necessary, a secondary fan below the main fan is incredibly useful. This secondary fan cools the plastic that has already been laid. The quicker the plastic can be cooled, the quicker it can retain its structural stability. This helps the plastic keep its rigidity when more plastic is laid on top of it. If the

Eyeglass frames are one of the more interesting and functional projects you can make on a 3D printer.

general consensus to give the build plate a healthy, thick coat of hairspray to make sure the build plate is incredibly sticky. Moreover, it is important that the amount of hairspray is relatively consistent throughout. Consistency is important when dealing with the build plate. If any section of the filament does not adhere to the build plate, it can be pulled up by later layers being laid. This will create errors and imperfections in the 3D print or ultimately cause it to fail and become filament spaghetti.

The third and safest option is using a layer of glue on the build plate to maintain layer adhesion. It is important that the glue you use is washable so it can be cleaned easily from the build plate. Using a glue stick and making consistent strokes throughout the build plate will make a strong layer of adhesion. This is especially good if you do not have a heated bed. The gooey nature of the glue will automatically bind to the filament and keep it fixed well. However, if you are using a heated bed, the heat from the bed will dry out the glue during the first layer. This can become a major issue if there is not a good amount of glue on the build plate. The dried glue will do no more good than the build plate's regular surface. The best feature of the glue is freeing the 3D print from the build plate. With painter's tape and hairspray, the 3D print will still be very close to the build plate and will be incredibly hard to remove. However, by spraying the build plate lightly with water, the glue will become viscous again and allow for the 3D print to be freed more easily than the other methods. Moreover, if you spray the build plate with water after printing, then a putty knife can be used to scrape away the residual glue. This is incredibly satisfying and helps keep your 3D printer clean. Make sure you don't spray the rest of your printer with water, however, or you could risk rusting or electrical problems.

Another great tool to help first layer adhesion is a flexible build plate. Many build plates are removable, and this can help with the adhesion process. If you have a removable plate, you can wrap it in blue tape, spray it down with hairspray, coat it with glue, or any

Glue rinsed with water can be scraped away from the build plate using a putty knife.

combination of the three. You can put the build plate back onto the printer without potentially damaging the printer with residual glue, hairspray, or tape. A very good material for your build plate is glass. Using glue sticks on a glass build plate will ensure that your first layer will both adhere to the build plate and be smooth. The smooth properties of the glass will allow the filament to become just as smooth and satisfying on the first layer.

A lot of flexible build plates come with bumps and grooves, which allow the filament to stick well to the plate. But the most useful feature is that they can be bent easily. When removing a model from the build plate, you usually need to use a putty knife to chisel the base of the print. Once the knife has worked its way under the print, you need to apply pressure upwards, freeing it from the plate. This is slightly easier with a removable plate because the plate can be set to whichever angle lets you best leverage the 3D print off the plate. But by far the easiest way to remove a 3D print is with a flexible build plate. Once removed, the plate can simply be bent, causing the model to snap right off. If you have a very brittle print that might be compromised by the bending of the plate, we do not recommend removing and bending the build plate. But for all other prints, bending the build plate will free the print easily with no compromise to the model. Instead of chiseling away at the model and potentially damaging it, bending the build plate releases the surface cohesion the model has on the plate and releases the entire surface area of the model

A 3D-printed ninja star must be carefully and deliberately removed from the build plate with a putty knife.

from the plate. This does not happen instantly or quickly with larger prints on a rigid build plate.

All of these tools can help you print more effectively with PLA. Because of its low melting point, it can benefit immensely from a secondary fan, heated bed, and build plate accessories (like different beds, tape, glue, and hairspray). And because of how agreeable it is with several methods of printing, it is the most widely used 3D printing plastic. Moreover, it works so well under differing conditions that filament manufacturers are testing its limits and potentials. PLA's most major and interesting advancement is in **material mixing**.

Adding Attributes

Material mixing is the process of adding an additional material to the plastic to give the plastic different attributes. Some major examples of this are silver, aluminum, and gold PLA. These are types of PLA that have flakes of metal in them. These flakes can give your prints a different look and are especially useful when making jewelry. The process of creating this mixed PLA is fairly simple. Filament is created by melting beads of plastic into a funnel. Once melted, the PLA stretches and becomes a strand. This strand is then cooled and coiled. Usually the plastic is coiled right onto the spool so it is ready for printing. This same process is used for making PLA, ABS, PETG, PVA, and flexible filament. The main difference between creating spools of PLA and mixed-material PLA is in the melting process. Instead of only using PLA, bits of other materials are added to the PLA.

3D PRINTING TIP

You can weld 3D prints together using friction welding. To do this, insert small filament pieces into a Dremel (rotary saw) or drill gun. Spin it incredibly fast as you press the filament into the gap between the pieces you are welding. The filament melts because of the friction between it and the plastic pieces. Pull the filament from the front of your two pieces to the back and you will weld them together.

This causes the PLA to mix and form a new consistency with the added material. PLA is the best plastic for this process because of its low melting point. Since it melts at a low temperature, the additive material can also have a low melting point. Some other filaments need higher melting points to be usable, which can damage the additive material.

One thing to watch for is that PLA will distort more easily than other plastics when exposed to heat. It can warp when exposed to direct sunlight. This also makes it a bad choice for a container that will hold heated items. Do not use it to hold hot foods or tea because PLA is not food safe. Also, PLA should not go in a dishwasher.

Just like gold and jewelry, not all of this filament is made purely of one material. In jewelry, this is known as karat, and it dictates the purity, rigidity, and price of the metal in the jewelry. Filament is no different. However, the main reasons for the concentration of differing material is structural integrity and cost. There should be no more than 40 percent additive material in the mixed-material PLA. If there is more than 40 percent, the filament will lose its strength and become brittle. This might not seem like an issue for the final product, but brittle filament is damaging to the 3D printer's extruder. Brittle filament can cause jams and warping of the extruder if the printer is laying filament poorly.

Even with a good ratio of mixed material to PLA, the filament can still become brittle. This is usually due to improper storage of any filament. The best practice for keeping filament in working condition is to make sure it is in a dry place. Humidity affects the cohesion of the plastic and will cause the filament to be less effective. If you do not have a dry area in your work space, or if you live in humid places such as Florida, it is a good idea to use silica gel. Silica gel is a desiccant, or dehumidifier. These are the gel pellet packages that come with beef jerky, shoes, and other dry products. They usually have printed on them, "Do not consume under any circumstances." This is good advice: silica gel is highly harmful to people. However, it is perfect for filament. If you have opened a new package of filament, you have probably noticed that it comes packaged with a silica gel bag. If not in use, it is a good idea to keep your spools of filament in either a box or bag with silica gel to keep it dry and ready for printing.

We recommend saving silica gel packages from dry food purchases so you can keep them for your filament. However, there are microwavable silica gel pellets you can purchase online that will dry out when microwaved so they can be reused. If all else fails and you need a dehumidifying solution in a pinch, cat litter also works.

3D PRINTING TIP

Filament can also be used to add features to your 3D prints. Some 3D modelers make a small hole in their models that is the size of their filament. Once the 3D model is finished, the creator can clip off a strand of filament and insert it into the finished 3D print. This can create a hinge for the print, give accent colors to the print (by using different-colored filament), and more.

The same properties that are used to absorb odor and liquid from cats help dehumidify your filament. Keeping silica gel near your stored filament is recommended for keeping your filament usable for as long as possible.

Maintenance Kit

Having covered the basics of how the 3D printer works, we know that there are certain parts of the 3D printer that require maintenance. You might have noticed that in maintaining or repairing the extruder nozzle, *x* movement section level, and filament jams we needed some tools to help the process. Tools are essential to working with a 3D printer. Not only is it important to have tools to repair and tweak a printer, it is imperative to have tools and materials that help you set up a 3D print and remove the 3D print from the 3D printer.

All of these filaments that we have covered are additive. This means that they add plastic to the build plate to create a model. However, there is another way to create a 3D print called **subtractive manufacturing**. This is when a material is dug into or drilled to create the model. The most popular versions of this use CNC machines. These machines are not commonly found in schools.

The type of 3D printing called CNC milling is far less expensive and can give a great result. CNC stands for "computer numerical control." This means that a small computer controls the motors and drill of the

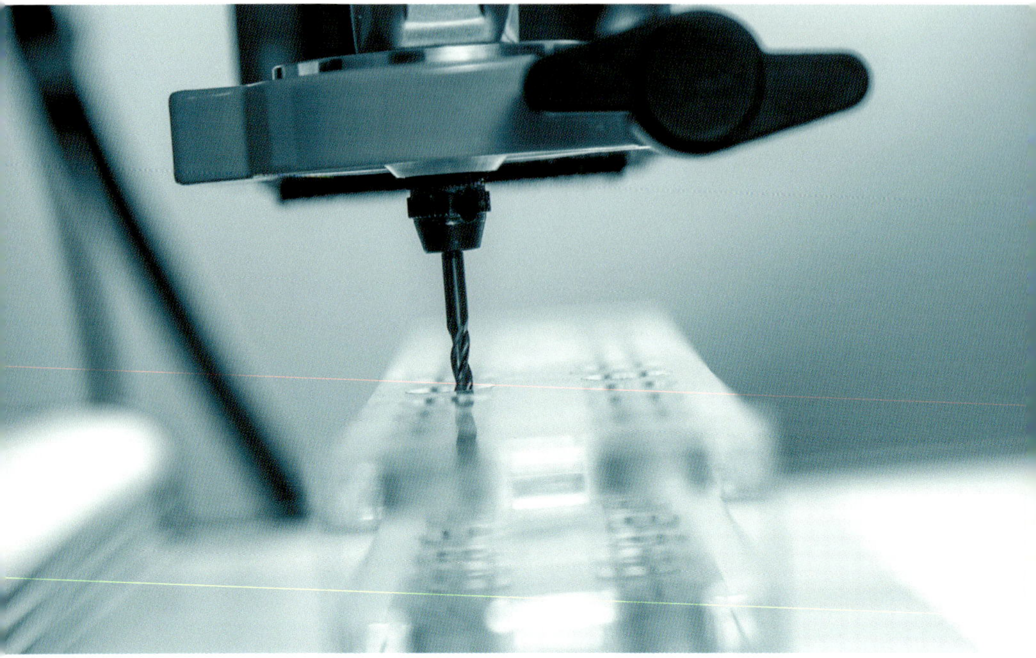

A CNC (computer numerical control) machine is subtracting material by drilling into a block of clear acrylic.

machine. Just like a 3D printer, it uses a small computer to drive motors and work over a build plate. Both the CNC machine and 3D printer use *x* and *y* coordinates to know where a design must be constructed. However, the main difference between CNC and 3D printing is that a CNC does not use the *z* axis. CNC machines use a drill bit to make a controlled drill into the material. This is the subtractive quality of the CNC. It subtracts from the material that is attached to the CNC's build plate. By utilizing little of the *z* axis, the CNC machine can create a quick product. CNC machines are very good for etching and embedding a design into a surface. Some have used

CNC machines to etch logos and messages into the back of their phones or laptops. This is easier than 3D printing and has far more **constraints**, but it can be interesting and convenient.

Another form of 3D printing not usually found in schools is powder printing. Powder printers shoot lasers into a large block or a layer of powder. The powder is hardened by the laser. Once the printing is done, the residual powder is vacuumed away, and the newly sculpted design is treated to keep it solid. This type of printing is incredibly accurate but extremely expensive. Powder printing can also add color to your prints.

Colored ink packets in yellow, cyan, and magenta stain the print and can give the model very vivid colors. These three colors can cover the entire RGB color range. RGB stands for “red green blue.” In digital terms, these are the three colors (red, green, and blue) which, when mixed, can give you any other color on the color spectrum. By adding red and green you get yellow, by adding green and blue you get cyan, and by adding blue and red you get magenta. Conversely, you can add cyan and yellow to get green, yellow and magenta to get red, and magenta and cyan to get blue. Just like red, blue, and green, yellow, magenta, and cyan can create any color when mixed in different amounts. By using these yellow, magenta, and cyan color packets, the powder printers can create colorful 3D prints whose colors are dictated by the 3D model or textures that are overlaid on the model in software.

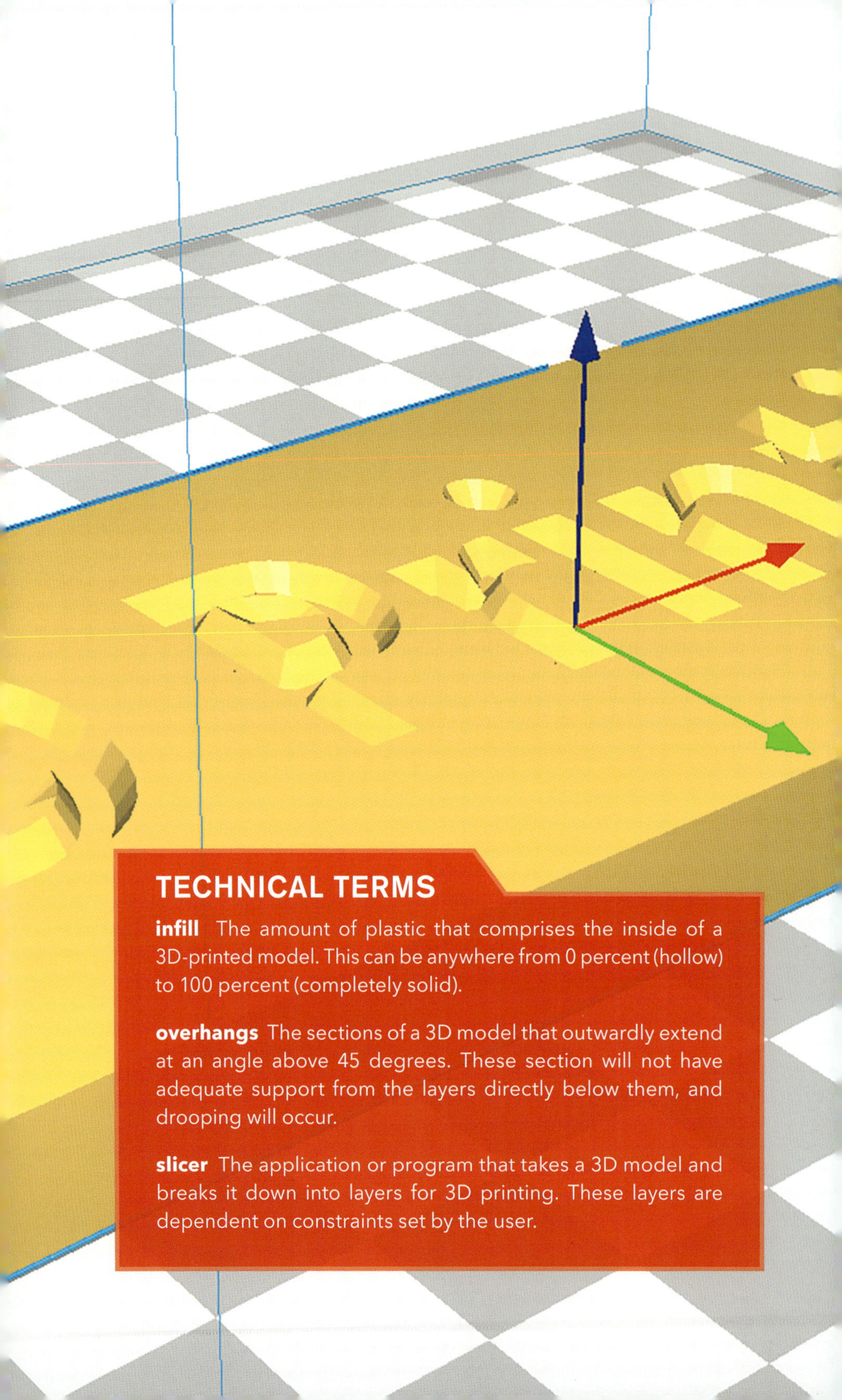

TECHNICAL TERMS

infill The amount of plastic that comprises the inside of a 3D-printed model. This can be anywhere from 0 percent (hollow) to 100 percent (completely solid).

overhangs The sections of a 3D model that outwardly extend at an angle above 45 degrees. These section will not have adequate support from the layers directly below them, and drooping will occur.

slicer The application or program that takes a 3D model and breaks it down into layers for 3D printing. These layers are dependent on constraints set by the user.

CHAPTER FOUR

Slicing Your 3D Model

WHAT DOES SLICING HAVE TO DO WITH 3D PRINTING? The way that you prepare a 3D-printed model is through what is known as a **slicer**. A slicer is a computer program that interprets a 3D model. The 3D model is imported into the application. The user then sets several settings that he or she wants the final model to have. Then the slicer slices the model into very thin layers. These layers will make up the final 3D-printed model. The slicer creates these layers because the 3D printer lays down the plastic in strands. These strands of plastic create a layer, and then the layers combine to make up the final 3D print. Most slicers have a view

Opposite: You can control the font, bevel, and depth of your letters using the text option in Tinkercad.

setting that will show all the layers of the 3D-printed model, as well as the path that the 3D printer will take to lay down those layers. This is incredibly useful if the user wants to troubleshoot where a 3D print might be failing.

So let's get slicing. The first thing you'll want to do is get a 3D model to 3D print with. This can be something that you have drafted yourself or something you found online that you want to print. If you are doing your first models in school or in a makerspace, find something online to print to get started. This will allow you to get familiar with the software before you spend time customizing your own project.

There is one other consideration. Many people will be using the 3D printer at the makerspace. Therefore, you should have your design ready before you get to the makerspace. If you are tinkering with your design during your time with the printer, you will lose valuable printing time. You might also be unintentionally monopolizing the 3D printer so others can't use it.

We will cover an excellent online model resource later. However, it is also incredibly satisfying creating your own 3D model to print. So, as a quick introduction to 3D modeling, we will be modeling your name. We will make this model using two quick and easy tools to create your own 3D models for first-time printing. Both of these tools are free; however, one is online, and the other requires a Windows 10 operating system or higher. These tools are useful for further 3D printing and advanced methods to create 3D prints and 3D models.

Free Modeling Software

Our first 3D modeling tool is Tinkercad. You can access it at the Tinkercad website (https://www.tinkercad.com). You can link your designs to either a Facebook or email account so your 3D models can be accessed later. Once you've created an account, the site will take you to your account page. Click on the Create New Design button, which will take you to the 3D modeling environment.

When you do this, notice that there are several shapes on the right side of the screen. This is part of Tinkercad's insertion section. These are tools that help you insert premade 3D models. You will be writing your name on one of the shapes. Once you select one of those shapes, you can place it on the 3D environment by clicking somewhere on the 3D base. Use the edges and sides of the shape to move it and change the model's shape and size. Hold the right button on your mouse to reorient the 3D space and change your viewing angle of the 3D model. For any manipulation you make to the models that you don't like, simply press the ctrl + Z keys (or cmd + Z for a Mac) to undo your last few manipulations. When editing these shapes, make sure that your shape is bottom heavy (having lots of area on the environment base).

Once you are content with your shape, you will add the text for your name over it. Click off of your shape by clicking anywhere outside of your shape. This will deselect your shape so we can move on. You can also

3D PRINTING TIP

Tinkercad has an amazing import feature. First you turn a photo or an illustration into an SVG file. An SVG file is a scalable vector graphic of an image. You can then import the SVG into Tinkercad. You can scale your project, and Tinkercad will generate an accurate, printable 3D model of your 2D design.

achieve this by pressing escape on your keyboard. From the same panel on the right where you selected your shape, click on the drop-down menu that says "Basic Shapes." The menu will drop down, and you can select the option "Text." You will then see a selection of letters. You can either select the letters that make up your name from those options, or you can select the icon that says "Text." This is an image of a 3D-modeled word "TEXT." If you select the Text option, simply place it on the 3D environment the same way you placed the shape. Once you've placed it on the environment base, a small menu (to the right of the Basic Shapes and Text menus) will appear. Using this menu, you can adjust the text, font, height, bevel, and segments of your text 3D model. Simply type in your name and preferred font. You can also manipulate the height, bevel, and segments of the 3D model to your liking. If you use the Bevel tool, each edge of the word will have a slanted surface. This gives the design more complexity and can make your 3D print look more professional.

Once you have the text object of your name ready, it's time to add it to your shape object. You can do this by selecting your text object. You will see the same options and points that you could use to manipulate your shape. Use the arrow pointing up to pull the text object off the 3D base. Now that the text is elevated above your shape object, we need to place it on the shape object. Move your camera view above the 3D base so you are viewing the two objects from an aerial view. Then simply click and drag your text over your shape. Move and stretch your text over your object to your liking.

Once your text is over your object, let's make sure it will print properly. Set your camera view to a profile view (looking at the models from the side). Now select your text model. You should see a small square below or above the arrow we used to pull the model off the 3D base. This square will stretch the model up or down (giving it depth). Stretch your text model up or down to merge or overlap with the shape model. And now you're done! Simply click the Export button on the right-hand menu panel, select "Everything in the design," and choose the **STL format**. You can now download your 3D model to your computer so we can print it. Make sure to put it somewhere you'll remember, like your downloads or desktop folder.

Tool for Windows

Let's move on to another useful tool called 3D Builder. This is a free tool in Windows 10. To open it, click on the Start menu in the bottom-left corner of the screen.

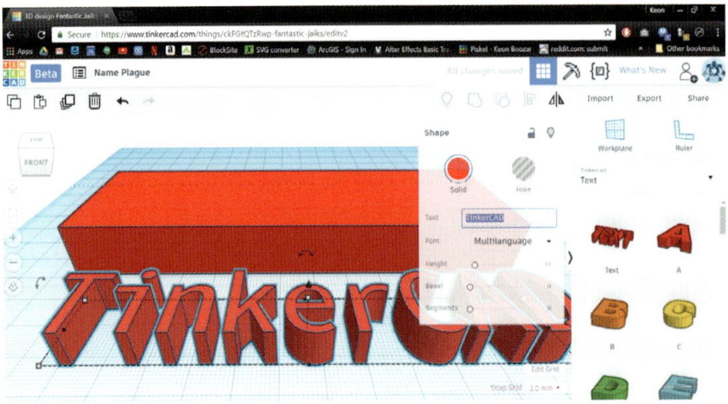

The user interface and 3D environment of Tinkercad are seen here, with letters before they have been placed on the shape object.

Then type in "3D Builder," and the 3D Builder logo should appear. It is a small rectangular arch that looks hollow and has a small, segmented triangle on its right side. Select that application, and it should open up into a selection window. This window should have the logo in the left corner, a few options on the left, and several models on the right. The models on the right are free, completely modeled items that can be printed straight away. They are incredibly well designed. The selection on the right has several categories of models, and many will print well right away. To create our own 3D model, we will select the New Scene button on the left menu.

Here you will see a 3D environment similar to Tinkercad. You'll also notice an option bar at the top of the screen. This is where the magic happens. We will be selecting the Insert option. This will open another bar above with several shapes. Select one and it will appear in the 3D environment. At the bottom of the window are three useful tools. These are the manipulation tools. The arrows let you move the object up, down, left, right, forward, and back in 3D space. The circular arrow lets you rotate your object, and the box with arrows going out helps you expand and shrink your object in different ways using the arrows that appear on your shape when you select that tool. Select your shape and use the bottom tools to make something to your liking. You can also overlap shapes to create new, interesting shapes. You can subtract shapes from other shapes as well. If you have an object you found online that you would like to edit, you can also import it here and edit it using the Edit menu. Your shape should be something bottom heavy, just like in Tinkercad, to make sure it will print properly. You can also try other interesting tools in the Edit option above. Once you've created a shape you like, we will put your name on it. Unlike the Text tool in Tinkercad, we will be using a more powerful tool in 3D Builder. By selecting the Edit option above, you will see another option bar. The tools here help edit your model and help you tailor it to your needs.

The tool we will use is the Emboss tool. Click this tool in that options bar, and you will see a new options bar at the top and the letters "abc" on your shape. In the text box above labeled "Text," type in your name. You will then see the "abc" on your model change to your name. You can change the font and orientation of the text using the Font and Projection options above. By clicking on your model, you can move the text around to where you'd

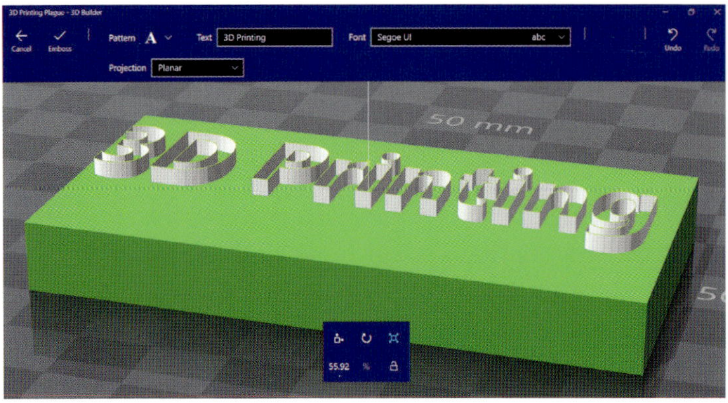

This is the user interface and 3D environment of Windows 10's 3D Builder program when using the embossing tool.

like it. In addition to moving it, you can use the double arrows around the letters that are projected away from the model to enlarge or shrink your text. Finally, you can use the arrow pointing out of the model to either push the text out of the model or embed it into the model by dragging the arrow down toward the model. When the text is to your liking, click the "Emboss" check mark in the upper left. Now your model should have your text embossed on it. You can now save your model and environment using the Save icon in the upper-right side (underneath the Close option, and next to the Undo button). When saving the model, there are two ways you should save it. First, name the file based on your model and keep the "Save as type" field as 3MF format. This is the file format for 3D Builder. You can reopen this 3MF file in 3D Builder so you can edit it later. Once you have that as a backup, click on the Save icon again and save your file using the "Save as type" option called STL

3D PRINTING TIP

3D Builder is a very powerful 3D modeling program. You can use it to "repair" your 3D models so they print well. You can make interesting designs with just the given shapes and models. And you can edit existing 3D models easily with the Split tool.

format. This is the standard 3D printing format that all 3D printing slicers accept. And now you have your 3D model ready for printing!

Model-Sharing Site

If you don't want to create your own 3D model, there are some great online resources that have hundreds of 3D models for printing. The site that we recommend using is Thingiverse (http://www.thingiverse.com). Thingiverse is a website on which people host 3D models they have created. As of the beginning of 2017, Thingiverse had a catalog of more than 765,000 3D models uploaded. These models vary in size, complexity, and detail. We recommend that you pick a relatively simple model to 3D print first, then move on to more complicated models. The simplest model that you could pick is a logo or nameplate. This could be a logo from a show, character, movie, or book that you enjoy. These are abundant online, and there are some very interesting ones on Thingiverse. If you do not want to print a logo, your name might be on Thingiverse. If you have a fairly common name, by typing in "[Your name] name," you might find a nice 3D model of

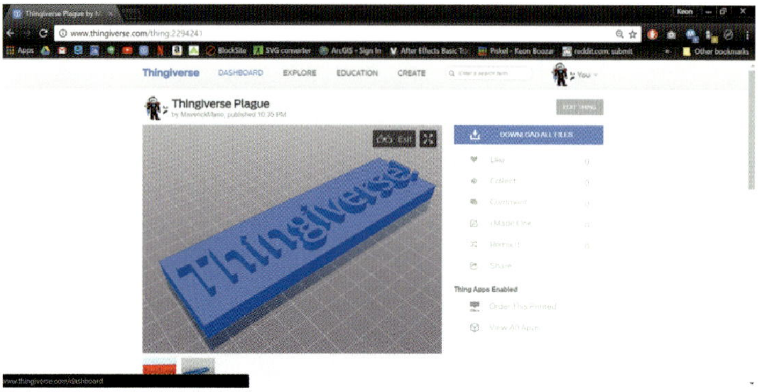

Thingiverse has a model for printing its name on its site, which also contains thousand of other projects you can print.

your name. These models would be similar to the models that we created in Tinkercad or 3D Builder. If they don't have your name, then you could create one in Tinkercad or 3D Builder and then submit it to Thingiverse.

Now that you have your 3D model in the STL file format saved somewhere you can access on your hard drive, it is time to start slicing. There are many slicers for different computer operating systems, each with its own benefits. If the 3D printer you are using recommends a specific slicer in the manual, we recommend using that slicer. However, all slicers should work similarly, and depending on your 3D printer's firmware, you might be able to use different slicers on your 3D printer.

The slicer we will be using is called Cura. This is a free slicer, and it has many incredible features. In our opinion, it is the best free slicer online right now. We do have a limited knowledge of slicers, but we have been using Cura and its updates for years, and it has never let

3D PRINTING TIP

You will need about 1 gigabyte of free hard drive space to install and run Cura, a free slicing program.

us down. If you are using a computer supplied by your school or makerspace, Cura may already be installed. If you are using your own computer, the first step in installing Cura is to go to https://ultimaker.com/en/products/cura-software. You can also find this address by Googling "Cura" or "Ultimaker Cura." Ultimaker (a 3D printing manufacturer) released Cura years ago and supports it on its website. Once at this address, click "Download for free." After you click that button, a pop-up window will appear. Simply answer the few questions about the purposes for which you are using this software, and it will allow you to download an installer.

Once downloaded, click the installer and follow the installation instructions. After a few clicks of the Next button, you should see the window called "Choose Components." This screen has the check-box options for 3D models that Cura can use. We recommend selecting all of these options so you can import and 3D print most standard 3D model types. The options to check are "Open STL file with Cura," "Open OBJ file with Cura," and "Open 3MF file with Cura." STL is the most standard 3D model file type. OBJ is another file type that allows for model manipulation in some 3D modeling programs. And 3MF is the file type for 3D Builder. If you have 3MF selected, then you can use the 3MF backup 3D environment file as your 3D model instead of the STL file. Finally, we recommend selecting "Install Arduino Drivers" as well.

Many 3D printers use what is called an Arduino board as a robotic brain for the 3D printer's motors. If you have this installed, Cura can use your computer to directly interface with the 3D printer. This will allow you to print without an SD card or other file transfer device. Once you have these selected, click the Install button and give your computer some time to install Cura.

Cura for Your Problems

Once the installer is finished, you will have Cura available on your computer! Open it either by using the shortcut on your desktop, by finding it in your applications menu, or by selecting "Run Cura" when you close the installer. Once opened, you will see a 3D environment similar to

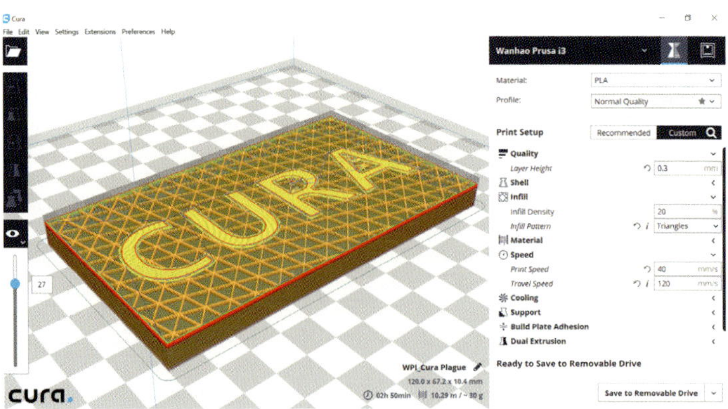

This is how the user interface and 3D environment of the Cura slicer application appears in the Layers View mode.

Tinkercad and 3D Builder, with two menu bars on either side of the environment. On the right bar are your printer settings, and on the left are your object manipulation tools. These tools are similar to the sides and edges you manipulated in Tinkercad or the tools at the bottom of the window in 3D Builder. If using your own computer, you need to create a 3D printer profile on the right that is made for your printer.

On the right, there are several fields that will dictate the constraints on your 3D printer. These are the features that will influence how structurally stable your print will come out. To create a 3D printer profile, click the Settings tab in the menu bar above, then go to the Printer drop-down menu, then click "Add Printer ..." This will take you to a window that has a list of printers. Try to find the model of your printer in the Ultimaker, Custom, or Other tabs. If you cannot, then Google the type of your printer or something similar to yours, and select that printer. In the bottom-left text box, you can name this printer so you can remember it. Then click "Add Printer" at the bottom. We will use the settings for a Prusa i3 as an example (since it has been the most popular 3D printer). The right side will then feature your printer's name, and the features for your printer are already in the fields below the printer name. These prefilled settings (under the area called "Print Setup") are the settings that the Cura developers have found to be standard. To make sure that these settings will fit your printer, first navigate to the Machine Settings window.

Click "Settings," "Printers," and "Manage Printers ..." Then select your printer by name and click the button "Machine Settings" on the right.

This new window will have the premade settings for your printer. Make sure they match the settings in your printer manual. For example, check the printer settings for the width, depth, and height. Together, these determine the build volume, which is measured in mm, or millimeters (there are 25.4 millimeters in 1 inch). Our Prusa i3 should have a build volume of 200 mm × 200 mm × 200 mm. The printhead settings dictate how much room each side of the build plate should be given for clearance. This will ensure that you are not too close to the edges of your build plate when printing. Finally, the gantry height should be set to 55 mm (allowing for 55 millimeters, or about 2 inches, of clearance for the top of the printer), and the nozzle size should be set to 0.4 mm. A 0.4-millimeter (0.01-inch) nozzle is standard for most 3D printers. We can now close out of these windows and return to the main environment. The other features that are incredibly important to your 3D print are the Print Setup options on the right. Let's explain these features and their uses in detail.

Quality Control

The first and most obvious setting is Quality. The best way to think about quality is to consider it the **resolution** of your print. Just like the resolution of your

TV screen and the image being displayed on the screen, the quality of your print is determined by how fine the details are. The smaller the quality value is, the finer the detail will be. The quality value, measured in mm (millimeters), dictates how thick or thin the layers will be. The thinner (or smaller) the layers, the more detail you can get from your print. The overall way to **visualize** this is that a TV screen with better quality has more pixels, so a 3D print with more layers has better quality. This value is dependent on your nozzle width, and your nozzle width will be dependent on your printer. This value can be found in your 3D printer manual. The quality value will be smaller than your nozzle width. For example, most 3D printers have a 0.4 mm nozzle. Therefore, a good size to print at is 0.2 mm to take half the nozzle area. The size at which you choose to print is called the line width. A fine-quality print can be printed at 0.1 mm with this 0.4 mm nozzle. A print that is large or does not need to have fine details (like a simple shape or a shape with a low polygon count) can be printed at 0.3 mm. The thicker your layers (meaning the higher the line width), the quicker your print will be ready because the model will have fewer layers. However, it will not have as much detail.

Second is the Shell feature. This is the thickness of the outer walls, or “shell,” around your 3D print. It is also known as the wall thickness. The rule for wall thickness is making the walls two to three times as thick as your line width. This will allow your printer to create two or three layers of plastic on the bottom, top, and sides of the print to keep your print strong. If you have thick walls to your print, depending on your print's structure, you might not need **infill**. This means that your print could be printed hollow while still remaining strong. So, for example, with our 0.2 mm line width, we should make our shell size 0.4 mm or 0.6 mm so there are two or three layers of filament on each side of the model. Therefore, both the fields named "Wall Thickness" and "Top/Bottom Thickness" should be at 0.4 mm or 0.6 mm.

The next and maybe the most versatile setting is Infill. This is how much of the inside of the print is filled with plastic. As we mentioned before, depending on your model, you might be able to get away with 0 percent infill. This will make your print hollow. If you want your model to be completely solid, then make the infill 100 percent. This is usually unnecessary. We recommend starting with 15–20 percent infill. This will fill 15–20 percent of your model with plastic. The infill is laid in a pattern inside the 3D print to give it rigidity without having to fill the entire inside with plastic. The default pattern applied to all prints is a square. This can be changed by going to "Settings" and "Configure Visibility." You will then see a large Setting Visibility list. Scroll down to "Infill" and check the box "Infill Pattern." In the infill feature section on the right, you will see the Infill Pattern drop-down menu with several options for patterns on your model.

Next, and most important, is the Material setting. Here is where you insert the individual settings for your material. This is the information we discussed in the

3D PRINTING TIP

When entering information on your filament, keep your flow at 80 percent. If you set it to 100 percent, your printer might have more of a chance of jamming.

previous chapter on filaments. Right below your printer's name (at the top right), you can see a drop-down menu called "Material." Here is where you will put what type of material you are printing with. Then go down to your Material drop-down under the Print Setup section we have been looking at, and put in the information for your filament. This is the information that came with your filament. Temperature is based on the ranges given by the filament you are using, and so is diameter. Finally, if your printer has retraction (which most do), check the Enable Retraction feature. This allows your filament to go back into the extruder and can cause fewer print errors and create fewer imperfections due to excess filament being extruded. Please revisit our chapter on materials for printing temperatures for certain materials as well as their pros and cons.

Slow It Down

Next we have the Speed feature, which refers to the speed at which the printer will be operating. These speeds are measured in mm/s (millimeters per second). "Print Speed" is how quickly the extruder will be moved while laying filament. "Travel Speed" is how quickly the extruder will be moved when not laying filament but moving from point to point to then lay filament. We recommend going slower to create a better 3D print. The standard speed is 60 mm/s, but reducing that to 40 mm/s will allow your plastic to settle for longer and ensure a solid layer. Travel speed is less important to the printing quality, but keeping it slower will allow the printer to keep its movement controlled and consistent. We recommend your travel speed be twice your print speed or slower. So if the print speed is 40 mm/s, the travel speed could be 80 mm/s.

Within the Cooling settings, you should check the Enable Print Cooling box. This will allow the secondary fan to cool your filament. This helps your prints with smaller layer heights or bridges that would be formed. However, if you do not have a secondary fan, then this section will not be used.

The Support settings are important but should not influence this simple print we will be doing. We recommend leaving the Enable Support box checked at all times. The slicer will calculate which angles of the model in the 3D environment are above 45 degrees. These are called **overhangs**, and these sections of the print could droop and cause print errors when being printed. Therefore, the slicer will create a small, simple tower that will hold up that overhang. You can see these supports by clicking on the eye on the left and selecting the Layers option. You can then see the 3D print layer by layer. This will show you the infill pattern as well as if there are any supports. It is always good to view your model in this layer mode before printing to make sure you know how it will ultimately be printed.

The Dual Extrusion and Special Modes sections will be left alone because they are for more advanced use. If your printer has a dual extruder, we recommend taking the time to understand its features because that is an incredibly useful tool. And with that, we have exhausted all the features. These settings will vary per printer, but we did a general coverage for the Prusa i3–type printers.

Load Your Model

Now that all the features have been tailored to your printer, we can load our 3D model. If you have booked time on a printer at a makerspace, you should have done all of this before your time begins. Click on the Open icon on the upper-left corner of the window. This will bring a pop-up file window. Navigate to the folder where you stored your nameplate 3D model, select it, and press "Open." Your 3D model will then appear on the build plate. Use the tools on the left toolbar (like in Tinkercad or 3D Builder) to orient your 3D print. The first option is Translation, or moving your print. You want your print to be in the middle of the build plate so it has clearance from all angles. The model will be sent to the center of the build plate by right-clicking on your model and selecting "Center on Platform." In this right-click menu you can also multiply your object to print several copies

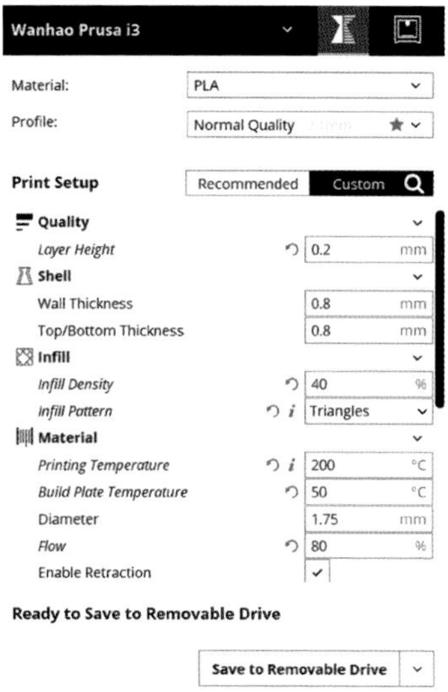

These are the recommended settings for a Prusa i3 3D printer in Cura.

of it. Or you can delete all of the objects on the build plate.

The second option is Scale. The beauty of using a slicer is that you can take any 3D model and make it as big or as small as you'd like. Just make sure that your print will fit on the build plate. The third option is Rotation. Use this tool to rotate your print. Make sure that your print has the side with the most surface area on the bottom so your 3D model will need the minimum amount of supports and will print the best way possible. A model with the most surface area on the top could become top heavy and need support to keep from falling. The fourth option is called "Mirror," which will let you create a mirror image version of your object. This is good for creating left and right versions of certain models. Finally, we have the Per Model setting. This will change the settings of your printer based on each model on the build plate. We do not recommend using this because your printer's settings should be set for all of your models to be printed as best as they can. However, you can experiment using this with models of different infills or other options. And with that, all you need to do is click "Save to File" on the lower right. This will save your model in what is called G-code. This is the language that the 3D printer uses to know the settings you have just established. All file names saved this way will end with .gcode. We recommend naming the file something that invokes the file's shape, then put the file's print time and grams of plastic used. These are the two numbers at the lower-right corner of the 3D environment. By knowing your print time and amount of plastic you will use, you can keep these in mind when printing. And by manipulating the settings we have talked about, you can decrease or increase both print time and plastic used.

There is one last thing to keep in mind. Hours of operation and the needs of others may limit the time you have to print your project. Also, some makerspaces charge you for the time and materials you use during printing, so make sure a project fits your budget.

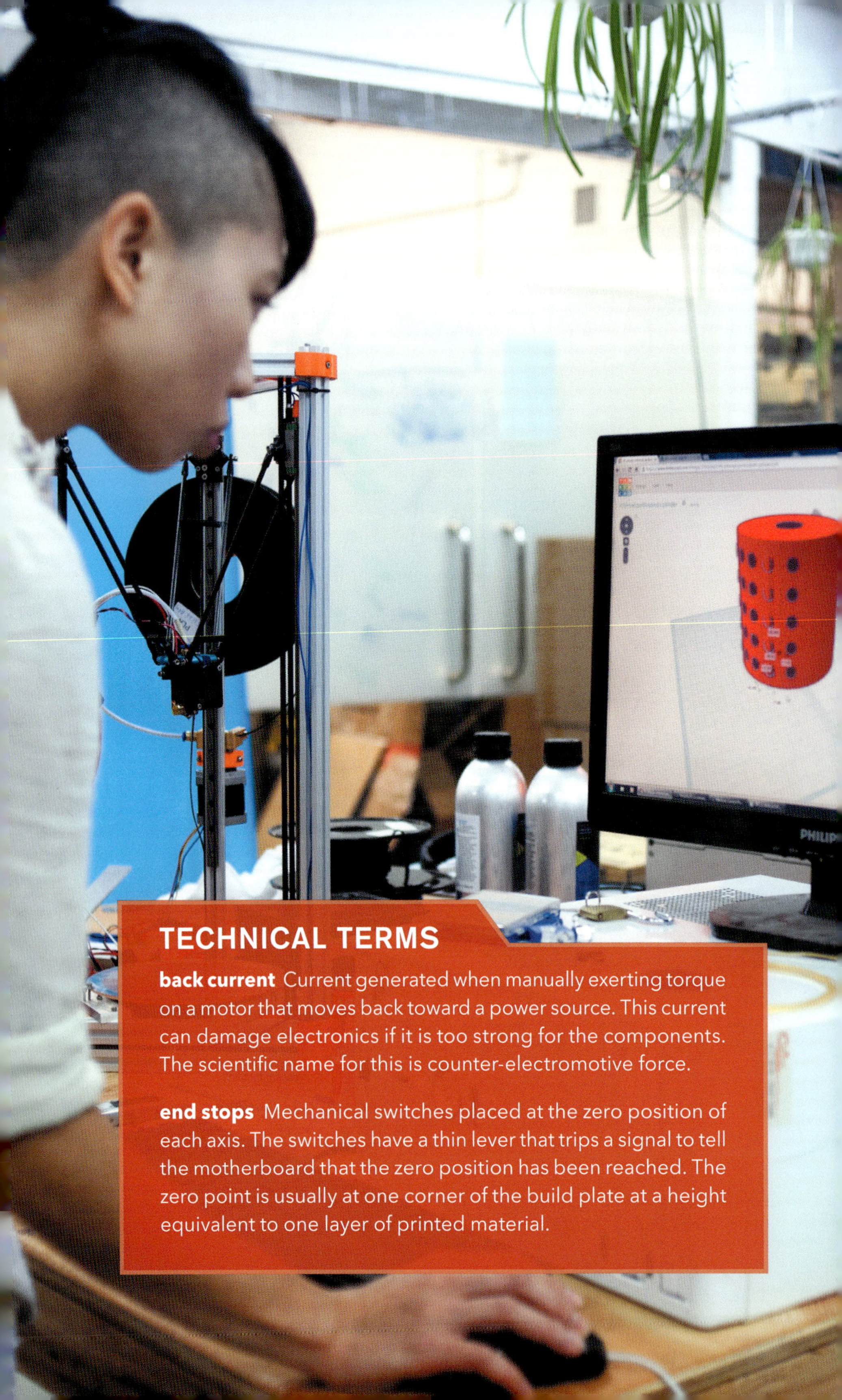

TECHNICAL TERMS

back current Current generated when manually exerting torque on a motor that moves back toward a power source. This current can damage electronics if it is too strong for the components. The scientific name for this is counter-electromotive force.

end stops Mechanical switches placed at the zero position of each axis. The switches have a thin lever that trips a signal to tell the motherboard that the zero position has been reached. The zero point is usually at one corner of the build plate at a height equivalent to one layer of printed material.

CHAPTER FIVE

Finally 3D Printing

IT'S TIME TO GET EXCITED. YOU HAVE PREPARED EVERYTHING to finally get 3D printing. You now are familiar with the background, tools, materials, software, and maintenance of your 3D printer! It's time to use that knowledge and learn a few more tricks to bring your first 3D model to reality. Since we have the G-code finished and ready to be placed on the 3D printer, let's begin with preparing the 3D printer.

Once you have turned on your 3D printer, you should understand the settings and features in the 3D printer's menus. We will be looking in depth at features in most Prusa i3 printers. These are standard on most

Opposite: Modeling software on a computer is used to prepare 3D objects for printing.

Become familiar with your printer's settings and have all settings entered on your laptop before connecting to your 3D printer.

3D printers. We recommend searching through your 3D printer's menus as well as reading through your manual for the printer ahead of time to make sure you are aware of what features your particular 3D printer has.

It is vital to ensure that your 3D printer is printing consistently on the very first layer. The first layer on the build plate sets the pace for the rest of the 3D print. We need to make sure that there are not corners that lift off the build plate, or any strands of plastic that are not set well, because if this layer ever comes loose, the entire model can come loose and fail. This is the initial part of the 3D print, so when the printer is starting to print, you can monitor and restart the first layer easily.

Starting Level

Repeat usage and doing something as simple as scraping a project off the build plate can cause the plate to get out of level. Therefore, it must be leveled regularly. Doing this will make sure that the first layer is strong. Some 3D printers can level themselves. Leveling the build plate is the process of tweaking the four points where the build plate touches the *y* movement section frame. If even one of these points is not level to the extruder, then the first layer will be inconsistent and could potentially fail. Therefore, you will need to have either manual control of your 3D printer's movement so you can move the extruder over each of these four points, or you will need your 3D printer to move to the four points itself using its motors.

In the 3D printer menus, there should be a leveling feature or a movement feature. If you do not have a leveling feature, use the movement feature to move the extruder to the farthest *x* and *y* coordinates and to set *z* to 0. If your 3D printer does not have this feature, or if you want to have full control, you can turn off the printer and move the extruder and build plate yourself. However, you need to make sure that your *z* axis is

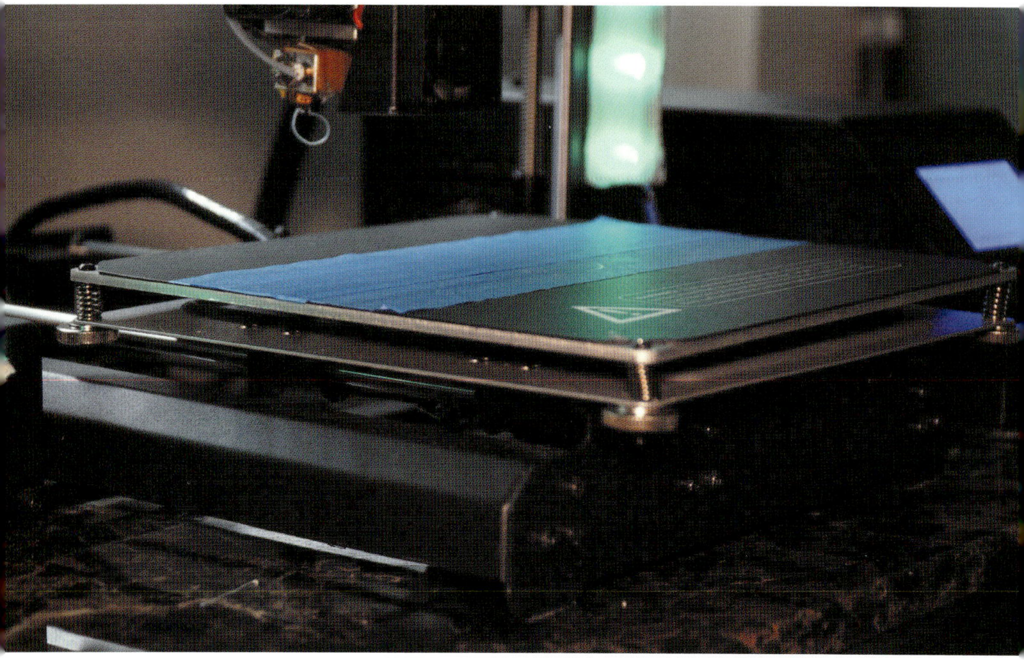

Knobs underneath the build plate are used to raise or lower the plate for leveling.

"home," meaning that it is at the 0 position. Be cautious and do not move the extruder or build plate fast. Move them slowly to the position you'd like. If you move them even a little too quickly, you can create a **back current** (also called counter-electromotive force). This is supplying torque to a motor that creates energy instead of spending it. This can be dangerous. Your 3D printer has delicate electrical components that can be fried if the back current is higher than they are designed for. So when moving the motors yourself, do it very carefully and very slowly. To safely move the motors manually, move them slower than your print speed. This is basically

10 millimeters (0.4 inches) per second, which is as fast as you would move a cup full of water to keep from spilling it.

3D PRINTING TIP

Before leveling your build plate, heat the plate to the required temperature. Materials will expand when heated and can change the distance between the build plate and your nozzle. Also, if you are going to put tape on your plate, add it before leveling the plate.

Once you have the *z* axis set to 0 and *x* and *y* set to "max," your nozzle will be at a corner of your build plate. Underneath that corner, there should be a screw with a spring separating the build plate and the frame. By loosening or tightening this screw, you can raise or lower the build plate. The distance between the nozzle and the build plate is one of the most important factors to first layer adhesion. The best way to level your print bed is tightening the screw until the nozzle has plenty of clearance, then loosening the screw slowly until it is very close to the nozzle but not touching the nozzle. The way to know that your nozzle is at a perfect distance from the build plate is by placing a piece of paper between the nozzle and the build plate. The paper should move beneath the nozzle with only slight resistance. No resistance means the nozzle is too far above the build plate, and paper that won't move means the nozzle is too close to the build plate. Once you've adjusted that corner, either move the build plate and nozzle manually or through the 3D printer menu to the other three corners. Repeat the paper measurement method to level the build plate.

The Right Gap

Now that you've leveled the bed, your filament will be able to sit strong on the 3D printer. When being laid, the filament should have a slight curve down to the build plate when moving. If the nozzle is too close, the filament will be squished on the build plate and can jam

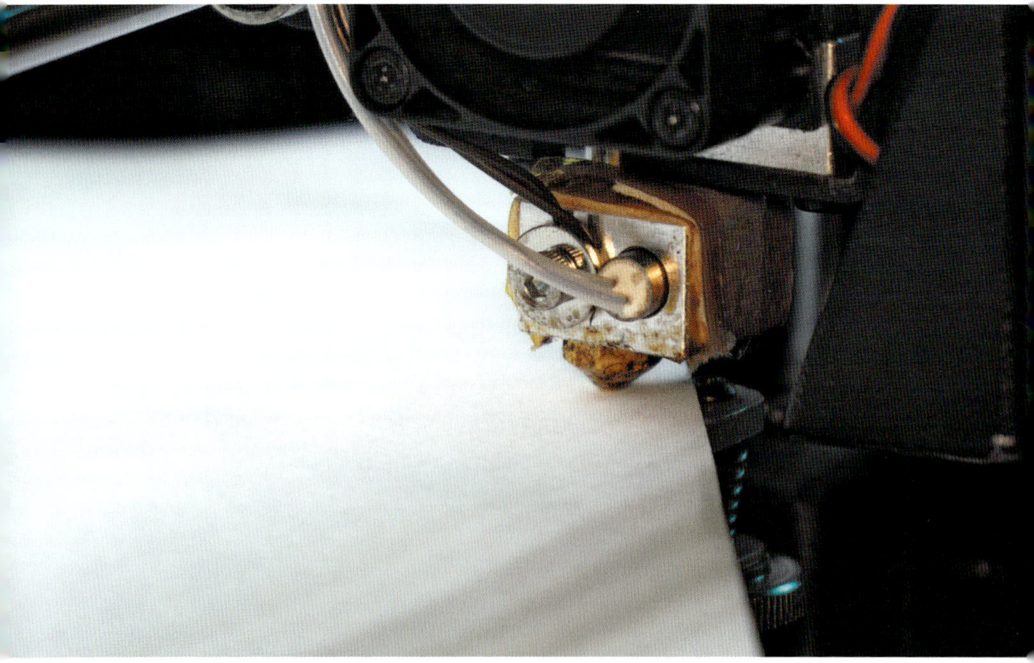

A piece of paper placed between the build plate and the nozzle should move with slight resistance when leveling.

the extruder. If the nozzle is too far from the build plate, the curve from the laid filament to the nozzle will be very severe. You will be able to tell it is not sticking because the filament will be round (not squished on the plate), show little detail on the first layer, and will not contour to the build plate (thus not gripping on it).

3D PRINTING TIP

Once you've started 3D printing, it is a good idea to print some upgrades for your 3D printer. Among these are spool holders, replacement brackets, tool holders, and more tools.

After the build plate is leveled, we can start preparing the rest of the 3D printer for printing. First we need to load the filament. In your 3D printer's menu, there should be a setting for preheating filament. Select whichever filament you will be using and allow the printer to begin preheating the extruder for that filament. If your 3D printer does not have these features, there should be a feature for setting the extruder and/or bed heat. Select the extruder heat and enter the printing temperature for your filament of choice. Allow your printer to heat the extruder to get to printing temperature. While this is happening, mount your filament onto either a filament dispenser or filament holder close to your 3D printer. This holder should come with your 3D printer and allow the spool of filament to spin, letting your filament be dispensed. Make sure that the filament is set the optimal way for the filament to flow. For example, if your spool is on top of your 3D printer, then make sure the filament is coming from the front of the spool so the plastic goes directly down into the extruder and is not going through a convoluted path to the extruder. This can cause the filament to snag and create issues.

In addition to making sure the spool has a direct path to the extruder, make sure that your filament is not tangled. This usually happens when a spool is not wound tightly, which can allow for the end of the spool that feeds into the extruder to go under another section

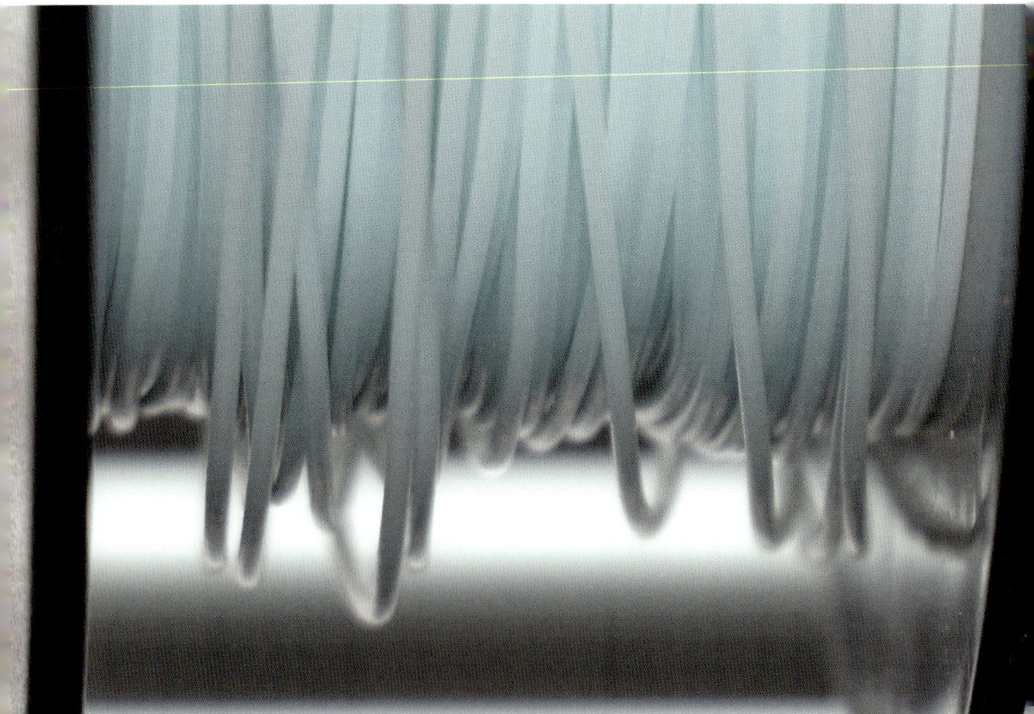

This tangled filament, which is improperly wound, can cause a snag and create problems during your print.

of the spool and cause it to overlap. This will become an issue after meters of the filament are pulled from the spool. This overlap will become stiff, preventing the spool from rotating and dispensing filament without high tension, if at all. The extruder assembly will then have to either pull harshly on the filament or not be able to receive filament. If it has to pull too hard, that can damage the extruder motor. And if the filament is tangled and cannot be pulled, then your 3D print will stop and not get finished. Then you will need to restart the entire 3D printing process. If the extruder stays heated without filament in it, the extruder assembly can be damaged.

Preparing the Plate

Even with perfect build plate leveling and a well-fed filament, there is a chance of the first layer failing and causing major issues. Here is where the accessories we have assembled come in handy. Before starting to 3D print, we recommend applying glue, hairspray, or blue tape to the build plate. You will need the thick blue tape we specified earlier. You should start from one end of the build plate and lay a long piece of blue tape over the entire build plate, with a little extra coming off both ends. If you are facing the 3D printer, you should place the tape from right to left or left to right. This allows the tape to be perpendicular to the *y* movement section (build plate movement). Therefore, if the build plate is moving forward and backward, the lines of the blue tape will allow for the filament to grip the build plate better. After that first blue tape strip, lay a series of blue tape strips parallel to the first strip. As you lay them down, make sure that they line up either slightly overlapping or very close together. For the best result, placing the strips as close to each other as possible without touching will make sure the first layer is consistent.

After you have covered the build plate, there might be an overhang on the last piece of tape you put down as well as on the right and left edges of the build plate. It is imperative that you use scissors to cut off all of this extra blue tape. Use the scissors to cut as close to the build plate as you can. If you do not do so, the tape can snag wires or sections of the printer. This can cause stress on the printer. Once cut, bend the frayed edges of the blue tape onto the sides of the build plate. This will keep the blue tape from peeling backward and potentially coming loose. Though this is a good fix for layer adhesion, if you are using a glass bed the blue tape will cause you to lose some impressive features the glass bed allows.

Glass-bed build plates do not need much help with first layer adhesion. Glass has a large, consistent surface that allows the filament to stick well on its own. If you do not use blue tape on a glass bed, you will find that the bottom (or first) layer of your 3D prints will be incredibly smooth. This is because of the smoothness of the glass, and it is very satisfying. Instead of blue tape, we advise using either glue sticks or hairspray for glass beds to ensure smoothness.

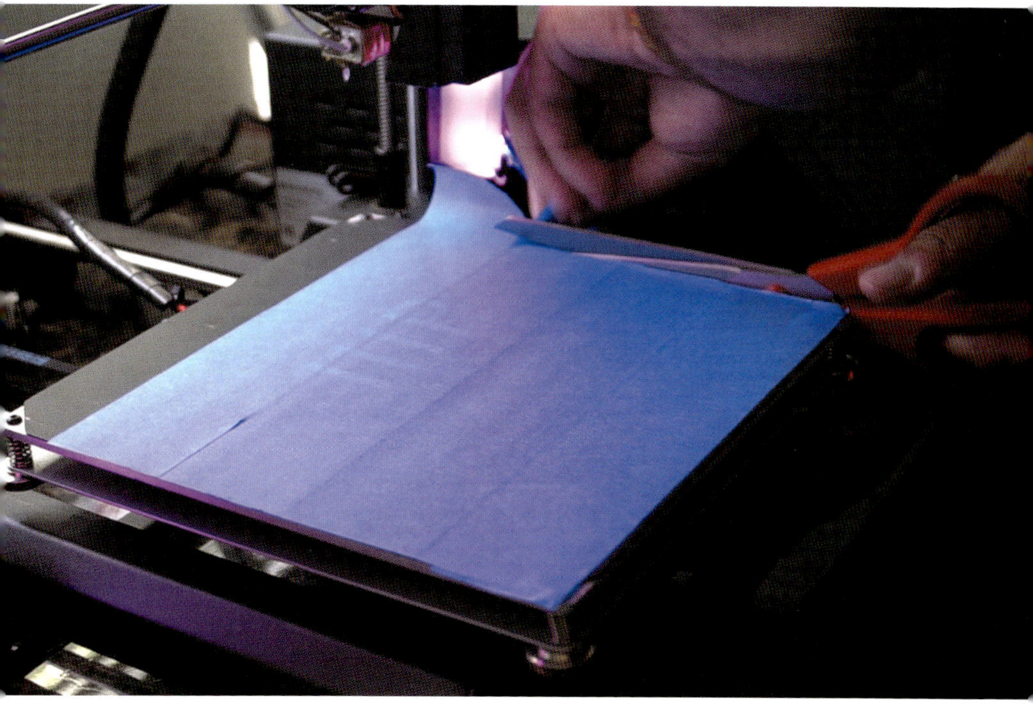

Apply blue painter's tape perpendicular to the build plate's movement and cut away any excess tape.

Hairspray is a good option for a glass build plate. Regardless of layers sprayed, the layer of adhesion should be thin and let the plastic lay strictly on the glass more than anything. This separates the plastic and glass bed the least out of our three adhesion options. Before laying down the hairspray, we advise preheating the bed. You should only spray the build plate just before you start your print. This is so the spray will still be wet once the printing starts. If you spray too early, it might dry out. And if you spray before preheating the bed, it will dry out quickly as the bed heats. As we stated before, it is a good

3D PRINTING TIP

Putting a layer of glue or hairspray on the build plate can ensure the first layer of your 3D print sticks to the plate. Preheating the build plate prevents glue or hairspray from drying out before you can put down the first layer of your project.

idea to spray the build plate liberally with the spray to make sure that the plastic will stick well.

Just as with using hairspray, we advise applying glue sticks to the build plate after it has heated. This is so the glue doesn't dry out quickly. It is also easier to apply the glue when the bed is heated. This allows the glue stick to glide on the build plate like butter. A little goes a long way with glue, so a thin layer should do it. Though this layer is not as thin as a layer of hairspray, it is usually stronger than hairspray and should provide the best adhesion for the first layer. Make sure to spread the glue consistently throughout the build plate so all edges of the first layer have strong adhesion.

Ready to Print

With the bed leveled, filament loaded, and build plate sticky, you are ready to start printing. Insert your USB device or SD card containing your 3D model's G-code file into the 3D printer. Navigate the menus to the Print Model option (or something similar) and select your model. If your extruder and heated bed are already at their optimal heat for your filament, then your print

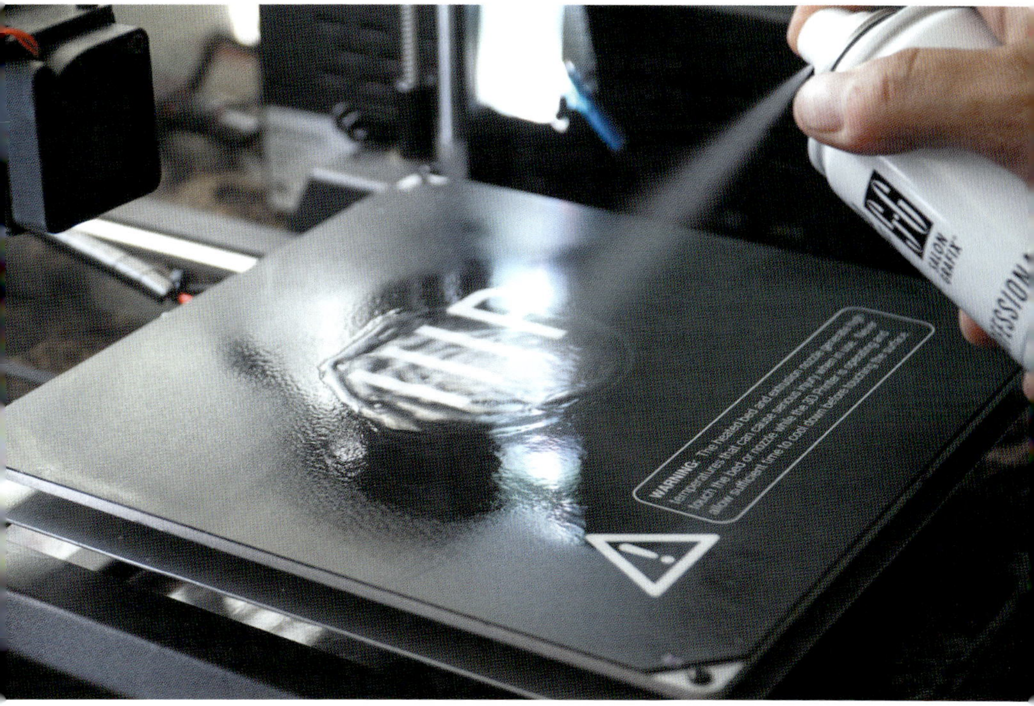

Liberally apply hairspray to the build plate just before printing for optimal adhesion.

should start right away. If your print does not start immediately, then your printer is probably preparing your extruder and heated bed for printing. Your nozzle will then move down the *z* axis and to one corner of the build plate. This is called "Home," or the 0,0,0 ($x = 0$, $y = 0$, $z = 0$) three-dimensional coordinates of the 3D printer. The printer achieves this by going to the three **end stops** of the three axes of movement. These end stops are a trigger at the very end of each movement section. By pushing the levers on the end stops and knowing where 0,0,0 is, the 3D printer can then assume that moving in the other direction along any of those axes will be a positive position. The printer then tells the motors to move to the positions that the G-code dictates and dispenses filament along the way. This is ultimately how the 3D model will be created and your 3D print will become a reality.

We definitely do not recommend leaving the presence of the 3D printer before the first layer is finished. If at all possible, try to stay near the 3D printer during the entire printing process in case something goes wrong. But since that is usually a very long time, it's understandable needing to leave the 3D printer alone. Applying the first layer usually takes from seconds to a few minutes; it is easy to monitor the 3D printer for that long before a several-hour print begins. If at any time during this first layer you see filament lifting or slipping from the build plate (not adhering), find the Stop Printing function on your 3D printer and restart the printing process. You might need to use more glue, hairspray, or blue tape to make sure the first layer is stuck well. Or you might need to check the level of the bed again so that the plastic is being laid in the slightly curved fashion we mentioned before. To be safe, you might need to move the nozzle closer to the build plate. However, this can be dangerous since it can cause quicker and harsher wear and tear on the nozzle, as well as jamming. Once the first layer of the 3D model is complete, you might notice that the previously off secondary fan will turn on. This means that the 3D printer is beginning the primary printing process. Since the first layer of the 3D model is stuck to the build plate, the filament will be able to stick to itself well in subsequent layers. Therefore, the rest of the 3D model should be fine for printing, and you can potentially leave the printer to finish the print. However, we recommend being close just in case there is an issue. Moreover, it is advised to keep your 3D printer in a well-ventilated area (especially if you are printing ABS, since it emits harmful fumes). Finally, make sure that your 3D printer is away from all **flammable** objects. As we stated before, elements of the 3D printer can get incredibly hot, so if something that can easily catch on fire falls on the 3D printer or enters that area, a very dangerous fire or damage can occur.

3D PRINTING TIP

When choosing a project to print, keep in mind how long you will have access to the printer in the makerspace. Make sure you will have enough time to print your project, remove it from the build plate, and clean the plate so it is ready for the next user.

Now that you have your 3D model printed, let's observe some things that might have happened while printing. When removing the model from the build plate, wedge your putty knife under the 3D model. Do not apply too much pressure, or else you can lose control of the knife and it can potentially harm you or something in the area. Lift the putty knife slowly to pry the model off the build plate. Depending on your adhesion aid, you can free your 3D print in a different way. If your 3D model does not have too much surface area on the build plate, you can peel back the blue tape to free the 3D print. If you used washable glue sticks, you can spray water around the 3D model, and that will allow the glue to become viscous and loosen the 3D model. If you have a flexible print bed, then simply remove the build plate and bend the plate to remove the 3D model. In any case, do not try to yank the 3D model off the build plate. This can break pieces of the model as well as easily put your bed out of level.

Removing Supports

When freeing your 3D model, be aware of supports that Cura (or whatever other 3D printing slicer you used) could have created. These are long, thin towers of filament that go from either the base of the build plate to an overhang or from a lower layer of the 3D print to a taller overhang. Though they can be removed easily, be very careful when removing them. If you yank your 3D print off the build plate and the supports are still attached, this can cause damage to the 3D model. These supports are made of the same materials as your 3D model, and they can be stuck to integral parts of your 3D print. Use your needle-nose pliers to break them off of your 3D print, and then use sandpaper to smooth out the surface that the supports were attached to.

Once the 3D model is free, look at it carefully. Look at the layers of the 3D model. If you cannot see the difference between layers, and the layers seamlessly transition into one another, then congratulations, your 3D model has perfect layer height and resolution. However, if you see that every layer is very distinct and they do not flow together, then that is a product of two things. If your layers are boxlike and come out in jagged edges, then this is due to the fact that your layer height is too high for the resolution you are looking for. If you are printing a **geometric** shape, high layer height is all right, but if your model is intricate and you'd like to keep that detail, then reduce the layer height. If the walls and edges of the printer are bumpy or in rounded edges when they should be smooth and consistent, this is a product of your print speed. Your printer is moving too quickly to lay the plastic and allow it to cool. Therefore the edges are being squished outward like marshmallow in gooey s'mores. A secondary fan helps this issue a lot since it cools the filament quickly. But if you reduce your print speed to between 20 mm/s and 40 mm/s, you should see a huge difference. If these two changes do not help, then this can indicate an issue with your motors. There can be too little or too much tension on your motors.

When you are learning to print, it is good to print one object many times, changing one variable before each print. Take notes on what you changed and what the outcome was. This will help you see the effects of each setting in your program.

Even if your layers have come out poorly, we can incorporate the help of sandpaper and a file kit to fix these issues. Rub your sandpaper around the edges that are rough around the outside of the 3D model. Make sure to do this over a trash can or garbage receptacle, and only do this in a well-ventilated area. Filament fibers can become airborne and potentially enter your lungs if not handled properly.

When sanded, the filament can become very small and become like dust particles around your area, so sand over a disposal unit. Once your 3D print is as smooth as you'd like, use the file kit to get into the nooks and hard-to-reach places of your 3D model to give it that nice finish.

3D PRINTING TIP

You can practice using the 3D printer while being useful at school. You can print models for use as visuals to help in the classroom. And you can help the drama club save money by printing props for the school play.

Work Skills

Now that you know how to 3D print, let's take a look at some fields you might be interested in that could utilize this talent. For anyone working with a 3D printer, it is always fun to make your own designs and 3D print them. Like with the 3D model of your name we made, creating your own 3D models can be incredibly satisfying and interesting. Moreover, once you get slightly more advanced in 3D modeling, you can make items to help you in your everyday life. Like we mentioned before, there is a wealth of models and information on Thingiverse and other online 3D model resources. But using 3D modeling and printing to make your own life hacks is a skill that can help any situation. Though we mentioned 3D printing a cup holder as an example earlier in the book, it is very useful to have holsters and containers you designed and 3D printed yourself to help organize your life.

In the same vein, 3D printing can help make tools that you can use every day. You can 3D print your wallet, headphone organizer, and even jewelry. 3D printing has an amazing presence and future in the fashion world.

These are among the myriad of items that can been created using 3D modeling and printing for school projects or to help at home.

Even now, fashion designers are working with CAD programs to make clothing and accessories that can be comfortably worn. They have even printed comfortable, moveable dresses with PLA. It is very easy to get started modeling bracelets, rings, and even earrings. In addition, you can improve a Halloween costume with 3D printing. Making a model of a fictional character's armor or accessories can help you get more into a character. The theater community does a lot of 3D printing to bring its characters to life.

In the engineering world, people are using 3D printing every day to create prototypes of devices. You can model and print housings for electronics with just some measurements and a clear idea of your final design. Civil engineers are even using 3D printing to visualize highway projects and buildings. For large-scale projects, it's usually up to the engineers to contract someone to make a scale model of that project. With 3D printing, the engineers themselves can make these models. If you are giving a presentation or doing something that requires visual aids, 3D printing can bring amazing life to your presentation. If you are talking about a building, then a small 3D model of that building to pass around can solidify a point. For a report on atoms or medieval technology, 3D printing can let you show or solidify an idea in real-live 3D that a Powerpoint presentation could never do. It truly makes your ideas into reality.

GLOSSARY

additive manufacturing The process by which a product or appliance is created by adding materials together. This is usually done by pouring plastic into a mold to create a plastic appliance. 3D printing creates objects by adding plastic or another material layer by layer to create a 3D object.

axis The direction by which something is moved. This can be: forward and backward; up and down; or left and right. An axis is similar to a dimension. The number of axes an object occupies is equal to how many dimensions that object has.

back current Current generated when manually exerting torque on a motor that moves back toward a power source. This current can damage electronics if it is too strong for the components. The scientific name for this is counter-electromotive force.

bearing A metal piece that allows components to move. The word originally refers to movement or relation. A linear bearing moves in only one axis or dimension (like a line). A circular bearing spins and can move with torque.

build plate The plate at the bottom of the build area over which a 3D printer moves and on which it lays plastic. By using motors and pulleys, the 3D printer can move this plate in two dimensions to create a layer. By moving the part that lays the filament upward to create another layer, the build plate can receive a three-dimensional object.

constraints A limitation of a process. Constraints on a program or a method are the maximum parameters in which a process can operate. In the case of 3D printing, the maximum size of the build space is a simple constraint. This constrains the largest size of an object that can be made on that 3D printer.

end stops The switches at the end of an axis of movement. When the extruder or build plate moves to its maximum distance in any of the three axes, the end stop switch is engaged, telling the motor it cannot move any farther. These are also used as an indicator of the 0 position. When all three end stops are engaged at the same time, the 3D printer is at its home position.

extruder The part of a 3D printer that moves on the *x* and *z* axes. It heats plastic to a melting temperature and dispenses this plastic for printing.

filament The plastic used for 3D printing. It is coiled onto a spool and fed into an extruder that meticulously dispenses it onto the build plate, thus creating a plastic model.

flammable Describing any object that can easily catch fire when exposed to heat.

frame The structure giving a 3D printer its shape. This can be made of sheet metal, acrylic, plastic, or metal beams. It ensures that a 3D printer can print with minimal extraneous movement.

geometric Made of angles, points, and lines; a figure that is made of smaller shapes to create a more intricate design.

heated bed A build plate that has a heating element underneath it. This element heats the build plate so it will accept plastic and allow it to adhere more easily.

infill The amount of plastic that comprises the inside of a 3D-printed model. This can be anywhere from 0 percent (hollow) to 100 percent (solid).

leveling The process of manipulating a 3D printer's build plate so that the extruder nozzle is at an equal distance from the build plate at any point it may move to during printing.

malleable Easily bent or shaped to fit a surface or position. Certain filaments can be more malleable when printing, which will ensure they stick to the build plate easier.

material mixing Combining base resins to create a compound filament for 3D printing. Mixing can produce filaments of different strengths and colors.

movement section An encompassing term for the assembly of parts and motors allowing a 3D printer to move on a certain axis.

open-source Describing original source code or software that is made freely available to be modified and distributed with no limitation.

overhangs The sections of a 3D model that outwardly extend at an angle above 45 degrees. These sections will not have adequate support from the layers directly below them, and drooping will occur. Thus supports must be created to keep these sections from drooping and ultimately to maintain the 3D model's structural integrity.

pulley A wheel that is turned by a motor to move a belt. This belt is attached to an object to push or pull an object. Pulleys on 3D printers usually are like gears that match teeth on the belt. The belt is attached to the extruder assembly and moves it on the *x* axis.

rapid prototyping The ability to create a work, item, or method that can be altered, modified, and remanufactured for use within a short period of time.

resolution The measure of the sharpness of an image or the visibility of detail seen through a device such as a monitor. Higher-resolution monitors show images in sharper detail than do lower-resolution monitors. Higher resolution in 3D printing is the result of thinner layers, creating smoother edges.

slicer The application or program that takes a 3D model and breaks it down into layers for 3D printing. These layers are dependent on constraints set by the user.

spool A cylinder that has a continuous strand of filament coiled around it, used to dispense the filament into a 3D printer's extruder for printing.

STL format "Standard triangle language," or the standard file format to digitally describe the layout of 3D objects. It is also an abbreviation for "stereolithography."

subtractive manufacturing A form of 3D printing that creates an object by removing pieces from a larger object rather than by adding to material on a build plate. Sculpting or die-cutting are good examples of this.

supports Small grid or tower designs that are created to ensure the structural integrity of a 3D print. These supports connect to overhangs to make sure the model does not droop in certain places and ruin detail.

threaded rods Rods of metal that have spiral grooves throughout their length. These grooves, called threads, pass through metal nuts with the same sized thread, raising or lowering the *x* movement section.

throughput The amount of material moving through a process or system.

visualize The act of illustrating a point or idea through purely visual means.

water-soluble Describing a substance that, when introduced to water, breaks down and loses its rigid structure.

FURTHER INFORMATION

Downloads of Programs and Projects

Autodesk Meshmixer

http://www.meshmixer.com

The homepage for a free 3D modeling and sculpting program from Autodesk (a large CAD program developer), which has powerful Voronoi tools and granular 3D sculpting settings.

Blender

https://www.blender.org

The homepage for a free popular 3D modeling program. Many use it to create video game-quality 3D models that can also be 3D printed.

Simplify3D

https://www.simplify3d.com

The homepage for a free 3D printing slicer called Simplify3D.

SketchUp

https://www.sketchup.com

The download page for the SketchUp modeling software. This site hosts several support documents for the program, as well as tutorials.

Thingiverse

http://www.thingiverse.com

A site that hosts user-made 3D models for free. You can upload files with different copyright parameters and engage in community communication.

Tinkercad

https://www.tinkercad.com

A free, easy-to-use site to create 3D models and download the 3D model you have created. We illustrate some methods of using this site in chapter 4.

Ultimaker Cura

https://ultimaker.com/en/products/cura-software

The download page for the free 3D printing slicer Cura (supported by Ultimaker).

Instructional Videos

Adafruit Industries

https://www.youtube.com/user/adafruit

The YouTube channel for a prominent electronics manufacturer. It publishes videos and tutorials on creating 3D prints that integrate electronics into the design.

CHEP 3D Printing

https://www.youtube.com/user/beginnerelectronics

A YouTube channel dedicated to testing, reviewing, and presenting consumer 3D printing technologies.

Dual Extrusion

https://www.youtube.com/watch?v=RE-ZgJ5vzXk

A tutorial video on using Cura and Simplify3D for dual-extrusion 3D print slicing and print prepping.

Make Anything

https://www.youtube.com/channel/UCVc6AHfGw9b2zOE_ZGfmsnw

An artistic 3D printing enthusiast with tutorials on using Solidworks to create 3D models, as well as many reviews and examples of 3D printing pens.

Maker's Muse

https://www.youtube.com/user/TheMakersMuse

A YouTube enthusiast who tests different consumer 3D printing techniques, materials, and printers to help hobbyists.

Replace 3D Printer Extruder Nozzle

https://www.youtube.com/watch?v=srS-95YtICg

A video describing the method to replace a 3D printer extruder nozzle. It also shows the differences between nozzles and their uses.

3D Printing Nerd

https://www.youtube.com/channel/UC_7aK9PpYTqt08ERh1MewlQ

A 3D printing enthusiast with many tutorials on 3D printing, examples of successful 3D prints, popular 3D printing trends, and 3D printing projects.

3D Printing Tip–Glass and Hairspray

https://www.youtube.com/watch?v=wzCcTCXGiDU

A video by the 3D Printing Professor about using hairspray on a glass print bed to ensure solid first layer adhesion.

Online Articles

"Conductive PLA." Proto-pasta.

https://www.proto-pasta.com/pages/conductive-pla

An article on conductive PLA from Proto-pasta. This filament can be printed with dual extrusion to create a 3D print that can carry an electrical charge.

Gaylord, Dave. "How to Clear and Prevent Jams On Your 3D Printer." MatterHackers.

http://www.matterhackers.com/articles/how-to-clear-and-prevent-jams

An article by a popular filament distributer that gives advice on how to keep your printer's extruder clear, clean, and jam-free.

"PVA Filament 3D-Printer Settings." Hestay.nl.

https://www.hestay.nl/en/3d-print-support/3d-printer-setup-per-material/pva

An article about printing with PVA, covering the settings to use and the features of water-soluble filament.

Stultz, Matt. "Fun with Flexible 3D Printing Filaments." Makezine.com.

http://makezine.com/projects/make-42/fun-with-flexibles

An article from Makezine (a maker community resource) that gives advice on the settings and steps to take when using flexible filament, as well as the mistakes to avoid.

"13 Tools to Help You Become a 3D Printing Pro." 3D Printing for Beginners.

http://3dprintingforbeginners.com/3d-printing-essential-toolkit

This short article covers some helpful tools that will allow you to use, maintain, and repair your 3D printer more efficiently.

Websites

Blender101

https://blender101.com/courses

A site that hosts courses for the 3D modeling software Blender. The site takes you through the steps to create video game-quality 3D models.

History of 3D Printing

https://redshift.autodesk.com/history-of-3d-printing

A timeline of the origins and current trends in 3D printing from a 3D modeling and printing news source supported by Autodesk (a prominent CAD program creator).

Shapeways

https://www.shapeways.com

A site with many helpful resources on subjects such as creating a 3D model, different printing materials, and the process of 3D printing. They also have a service where you can send them your 3D model and they will print it for you. They can even print the model in material you might have.

3D Printing Industry

http://3dprintingindustry.com/3d-printing-basics-free-beginners-guide

A beginner's guide to 3D printing from a reputable 3D printing news outlet.

3D Printing Materials (3D Hubs)

https://www.3dhubs.com/materials

An extensive list of 3D printing materials by 3D Hubs, which is a site that can print your 3D models using these materials.

INDEX

Page numbers in **boldface** are illustrations. Entries in **boldface** are glossary terms.

ABOUT THE AUTHOR

Keon Arasteh Boozarjomehri began 3D printing in 2012 through the Advanced Visualization Center at the University of South Florida. He then moved on to start his own 3D printing company named Print3D LLC. Since its inception, Print3D has created hundreds of 3D models, including custom designs for commissions, mass-produced items, and accurate costume pieces to support the local cosplay community. Keon now has a computer engineering degree from USF and 3D prints at least one item a day. He loves to spread the word about this exciting technology and pushing its limits.